VOICE
FROM THE PAST...

"Hello, Gilyan?" The connection was bad, but Gilyan, closing her eyes tightly and holding the receiver so hard her knuckles turned white, knew Jay's voice instantly. "Gilyan?" he repeated.

Over a tight throat, she answered: "Yes . . ."

"I wouldn't blame you if you hung up on me." Jay's voice came faintly.

She cleared her throat. "I won't hang up. What did you want?"

"I—I'm coming back to San Francisco in a week or so. May I—please—may I see you?"

Gilyan spoke almost sharply. "No, Jay! It would accomplish nothing . . . this call is accomplishing nothing. Goodbye." She hung up before the tears came.

The Waiting Heart
Marcia Miller

VALENTINE BOOKS
NEW YORK

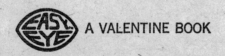 A VALENTINE BOOK

Valentine Books are published by
PRESTIGE BOOKS, INC., 18 EAST 41ST STREET
NEW YORK, N.Y. 10017

Chapter One

Gilyan sat quietly, but inwardly, a welling tide of happiness made it difficult to keep her fingers on the pen heliographing its way across the notebook. The brown-haired girl coming down the aisle in drifting white on the arm of her father wasn't a Miss Cynthia Carkenden; she was a slimmer, taller girl, with coppery hair and hazel eyes, named Gilyan Barr. The slender, blond young man waiting at the altar, his light-blue eyes fixed adoringly on his approaching bride, was a much taller man, with dark hair and eyes. And his name was Jay Hanover.

"I don't think your mind's on your work," a soft voice said into Gilyan's ear. Gilyan started and turned. Julia Caldwell smiled and held up her drawing pad to show her sketch of the bride's gown. "Pretty soon, Hannah and I will be cover-

5

ing your wedding, watching *you* walk down the aisle, sketching your gown."

Gilyan smiled back at the small blonde girl. "Now how did you guess what I was thinking?"

Julia's amber eyes, with the lovely slant to their outer corners, sparkled. "It wasn't in the least hard to do, Gilyan. Your eyes are dancing, your cheeks are flushed, and any moment—at least for the past ten—I've expected to see you air-borne!"

Gilyan muffled a laugh and turned back to watch the ceremony, concentrating. The concentration wasn't lasting. Within seconds, she found her mind singling out dates. This was September —the end of September, really—and Jay would be going to New York to cover a part of the World Series in a very short time. He expected to be away two or three weeks, and he said they could be married after his return. Late October? November? Gilyan's mind spun with dates, trousseau, a going-away suit, showers, bridal array, and all the silver-spun, moon-misted thoughts that have been a bride's prerogative since time immemorial. But to Gilyan, these dreams were unique, hers alone, a personal domain never entered into before.

It was only seven days back that Gilyan had discovered that Jay cared for her the way she cared for him. Their courtship had been sporadic. Jay worked for the rival *San Francisco Herald*, a sportswriter who, frustratingly enough, always seemed to be sent out of town on an assignment just as she was becoming confident that the feeling they had for each other might be a good deal more than friendship.

Gilyan had come to work on the Woman's Page of the *Globe* two years ago—fresh from receiving her Master's in Journalism—and was introduced to Jay Hanover three weeks later. Technically, as of a week ago, they were engaged. There was no ring as yet. Jay had bought himself a new car within the month and Gilyan was more than willing to wait. She didn't need a banded jewel as a symbol; that symbol she wore deep within herself.

In the roseate glow of her thoughts there were two minor gray spots. Her mother and father hadn't met Jay—a transatlantic call wasn't the most satisfactory means of making an introduction—and Gilyan felt a strange reluctance to tell Ardell Lewis, her roommate, that the engagement was official. The first small blot would be obliterated within a short time with her parents' return from London, but the second was more upsetting for the simple reason that there was nothing tangible, nothing that Gilyan could pinpoint. Ardell had never, by word or look, showed an antipathy toward Jay, but there was a withdrawal of her usual warm self whenever they were together, or when Gilyan discussed him. Gilyan faced the fact that she had actually been reluctant to force the issue. Idiotic, really. Ardell was the easiest person under the sun to talk to, and invariably considerate. It was quite simple. Tell her they were engaged. If there was an adverse reaction, ask her why. Theirs was a mutually tested friendship. It was nonsense to think—nevertheless, Gilyan had considered this—that it might be a form of jealousy on Ardell's part, or the fear that she would lose a roommate.

Julia broke into Gilyan's reverie with an exclamation. The bride and groom had gone back up the aisle and the crowded church was emptying. Julia consulted her watch.

"I must run. Would you be a darling and take my sketches back to the office with you? My aunt will be thinking I've been run over." The small, perfectly featured face clouded. "I should have called Aunt Grita before the ceremony."

Sympathetically, Gilyan touched Julia's hand. "Run along at once. Of course I'll take your sketches back with me." Julia cared for an invalid aunt who, more by what Julia left unsaid than by anything she said, must be a taxing burden for a twenty-three-year-old girl who needed to stretch a salary geared for one to two people, one of whom required expensive medication. Julia never complained; as a matter of fact, she seldom mentioned her aunt. The girls who worked with Julia respected her reticence; a sort of silent sympathy was the extent of their attitude where Julia's home life was concerned. Or lack of it. Her parents had died many years before and the aunt had cared for Julia until she became bedridden and Julia took over the household reins. These meager bits of information had been slowly gleaned over the two years Gilyan had known Julia Caldwell.

Hannah Davis, head of Gilyan's department, was at her desk, wrapped in concentration and a cloud of smoke. Gilyan smiled to see Hannah's elaborately flowered hat riding half off the gray-streaked brown hair. Hannah's grooming suffered only when she returned to the office to get her story down, or to answer some of the mountainous mail accruing from her column, The Question Box.

The Woman's Editor squinted mild blue eyes up at Gilyan as she waved a hand through the cigarette smoke to clear a path between them. "Ye Gods! Is it that time already?"

Gilyan laughed. "What time?"

"Another - wedding - under - our - belts time. I thought you just left." She lighted a fresh cigarette and Gilyan automatically reached to the ash tray and snubbed out the half-smoked cylinder still riding its overflowing rim. Hannah pushed at the brilliant, blue-flowered hat, and it slid to an equally impossible angle over the right ear. "Where's Julia? Did she make the sketches?"

Gilyan laid the sketches on the desk. "Julia had to get home to her aunt."

"Poor child," Hannah grunted, squinting at the pictures. "Good," she said. "If Julia could just write as well as she can draw." She raised her voice. "Elmer!"

Elmer, freckled face intent, hurried through the door. "Here—and here . . ." Hannah handed him a batch of copy, but Elmer didn't dash off as usual, and Hannah quirked a brow at him. "Something on your mind, Elmer?"

Gilyan knew. "Julia's through for the day, Elmer," she said gently.

The freckled face blazed crimson, but his voice was firm with offended dignity. "I was waiting for your copy, Miss Barr."

"I have to do a bit of proofreading, Elmer. Thanks, anyway. I'll bring it down." He mumbled something and shot out of the office.

Hannah snorted. "I'm about as observant as an ostrich with its head in the sand. How long has this been going on? I thought young Elmer had a crush on *you*."

Gilyan smiled. "My turn has come and gone. Right now, he's carrying a torch for Julia."

If he's so fickle at seventeen, what's he going to be at twenty-seven?"

"It's because he *is* seventeen, I think." Gilyan picked up her purse. "I'll get this Blake-Carkenden wedding whipped into shape and then I must run."

Hannah rubbed her chin and left a big black

smudge. "Sometimes I don't think I could manage without you."

"Come on now, Hannah, don't turn my head!"

Hannah gave her a fond look and rubbed her forehead, leaving another smudge that gave the lean, brown face, under the askew blue hat, a tipsy look. Gilyan called back over her shoulder: "Before you meet Roy, I'd suggest you look in the mirror."

Gilyan, behind her desk in her own smaller office opening off Hannah's larger one, laughed as she heard Hannah's distant whoop of dismay. Apparently, she had looked in a mirror. Gilyan knew that within five minutes, if she walked back into the outer office, Hannah would once again look like an elegantly slender fashion plate. At the social affairs she covered, Hannah often surpassed the guests in her grooming. However, on reaching her desk and typewriter, Hannah's dishevelment was practically instantaneous.

An hour later, Gilyan let herself into the apartment she shared with Ardell Lewis. It was a light, airy apartment high on one of California Street's hills and because of the warm yellow tone of the large living room, the grayness of many San Francisco days seemed shut away from them. There were two bedrooms, a bath, and a tiny kitchen of pink and white. The girls had looked a long time before finding the apartment.

A momentary pang hit Gilyan as she looked around the long, lamplit room with its yellow walls, and carpeting and plump chairs and sofa in the palest of green. Perhaps, if Cliff and Ardell married first, she and Jay could keep this place.

"Gilyan?" Ardell's head, wrapped in a thick towel, popped through her bedroom door. "You alone?" Ardell came into the living room wearing the quilted pink duster that made her round blue eyes look bluer and her cheeks pinker.

Gilyan smiled and started pulling off her coat. "I have to rush—get in a shower and change before Jay gets here," she said. She thought she detected a cloud cross the mobile face of her roommate, but Ardell sounded her usual placid self.

"Where are you two going tonight?" she asked, stifling a yawn, then bending to pluck a cigarette from a quartz box on the small end table.

Gilyan decided that she must be imagining things, guilty conscience, most likely, for not having told Ardell immediately that she and Jay were officially engaged. "Dinner and a show," she said. "Jay's leaving for New York in a few days."

She wasn't imagining things. As Ardell straightened, Gilyan caught the look on her expressive face, the swiftly concealed relief. "Oh?" Her tone was light. "Will he be gone long?"

Gilyan dropped the black cashmere coat and sank into a chair. Now was as good a time as any. Get this out into the open. She found herself stall-

12

ing by reaching out to the quartz box for a cigarette and lighting it. Then she slipped her feet free of the black suede pumps.

"I'm through in the bath," Ardell said, touching the towel. "I showered and washed my hair. Cliff will be over much later. He's doing some inventory for his dad." Cliff Wilton was a partner in his father's sporting goods store. Her tone suddenly alerted. "I—thought you were in a hurry?"

"Ardell, sit down a minute." For some reason, Gilyan's throat felt tight.

Ardell made it easier for her by speaking first.

"Is there something wrong between you and Jay?" she asked. The usually cheerful face looked serious, intent. Hopeful?

"Ardell—this is hard—" Gilyan floundered, then plunged. "Do you dislike Jay?"

The moment drew out, became much too long as her roommate, tucking the pink robe around her, sat down again.

Ardell snubbed out her cigarette and sank back. "This *is* hard—Gilyan—both ways," she said. "There are times when people ask your opinion that it should never be given. I'm afraid this is one of those times. To anyone else, I might be able to give the answer they wanted to hear. You—are something else again. I'm so fond of you . . ."

Gilyan swallowed over the tightness in her throat. "I—I think it's going to have to be said, Ardell."

The toweled head nodded. "If I'm jeopardizing our friendship for the lack of something like diplomacy, I'll never stop regretting it." Pleadingly, she looked at Gilyan. "Would you rather I had lied? Have said, Yes, I like Jay—when you asked me?"

Gilyan shook her head. "No. If there's anything —specific, I should know. You wouldn't be a friend if ... "

To Gilyan's relief, the toweled head was shaking. "Oh, no, there's nothing like that. You asked me if I disliked Jay. I know of nothing specific against him. Nothing actually that backs up my feeling. It's just ... " The rose-tipped hands flew out. "Darn!" Ardell ejaculated. "I didn't expect this. I didn't expect things to develop to such a serious point between you two, but I see they have."

"Jay and I are engaged. We plan to marry when he returns from New York." Gilyan leaned forward, frowning. "Why didn't you expect things to become serious between us?"

Ardell snatched the towel from her head and started rubbing the wet blonde hair as though it were an enemy she had cornered. "We've gone too far not to continue. Very well. I've always considered Jay an opportunist. I think he's a little *too* ambitious." As Gilyan's mouth flew open, Ardell raised her hand.

"Let me go on. Sometimes, Jay sounds like someone who uses people. Many times, when

14

we've all been out together, I've heard him say, 'Be nice to so-and-so; he could do me a lot of good.' Or—'Look, there's Mr. Such-and-Such; if I could get in good with *him*' . . . And money! Haven't you noticed how Jay acts toward people with money? How he talks about making it big for himself if he can just meet the right people? It sounds like he means *using* somebody to get ahead."

"But, Ardell, that could apply to lots of people. Take me, for instance! I got on at the *Globe* because Dad and the editor were old friends, cub reporters together, years ago. My dad wasn't *using* Matt Groody. He knew I was qualified for the job. It wouldn't have been fair to me if he had said—'Here's a job in a town Gilyan likes, a job she can do, but I can't recommend her because I know Matt.' "

"Oh, Gilyan!" Ardell exclaimed. "You're twisting what I wanted to say. Your situation has nothing to do with the opinion I've *reluctantly* been forming."

Gilyan controlled the anger she felt building up inside her. Ardell didn't understand that Jay wanted to better himself because he had always gotten things the hard way. Schooling and his first chance at being a cub reporter had been done without the help of anyone. His mother had died when he was sixteen and his father, obviously a man without any ambition, couldn't understand the drive in his son. Apparently, Ardell couldn't, either.

Selecting her words carefully, Gilyan tried to explain this to Ardell. How Jay had been on his own since sixteen and had managed to put himself through high school and college and then had come to San Francisco and started at the *Herald*. How he hoped one day to become a columnist, like her father, or The Lamplighter. That if he hadn't fallen in love with Gilyan, he would, most likely, have gone to Europe as a stringer for one of the press services.

Ardell's face cleared a bit. It was obvious she wanted to be proved wrong. "I never knew any of those things. They could explain what I considered—well, a mercenary streak in Jay." Her face clouded again. "Gilyan, has my being so frank hurt you, or our friendship?"

Gilyan rose, smiling. "Of course not. Friends aren't that if there isn't honesty between them. Now I feel better and," she glanced at her watch with a look of dismay, "if I don't get into the shower right now, I'm not going to make it."

In all honesty, Gilyan admitted she didn't really feel better as she showered and slipped into a thin silk sheath of clear blue, frosted with cotton beading. The words between Ardell and her couldn't be unsaid. As she fastened a short rope of blue and vivid green beads about her throat and touched the bouffed wings of coppery hair, the hazel eyes in their circle of heavily fringed dark lashes looked somber. She wished she hadn't forced the issue. Bringing the matter into the open had benefited no one.

Chapter Two

Because of her talk with Ardell, Gilyan's evening with Jay wasn't an unqualified success. If Ardell's invited opinion hadn't been expressed, Gilyan probably wouldn't have thought too much of two minor incidents that occurred during the evening.

She and Jay were discussing his pending trip. As Gilyan looked across the candlelit table, her heart caught in her throat. Open admiration was in her eyes at the sight of the smoothly planed dark face, the brown eyes under angled dark brows, and the cap of dark, wavy hair. Jay was, as always, extremely well dressed; linen immaculate and his suit beautifully tailored. She sensed that he paid a lot for his clothes, but took excellent care of them. As he caught her look, the white teeth flashed against the tanned skin. "I like you, too," he said.

Gilyan flushed. "Am I that obvious?"

He stuck out a lean hand and clasped hers where it lay on the tablecloth. "How many times have you been told how lovely you are?" He waved away her movement of protest. "No, really. You're beautiful, striking looking. Every time you come into a room, heads turn. Even the women's. I love it!" He looked extremely complacent, and for some reason, the compliment disturbed Gilyan rather than pleasing her. She felt as though she were being assessed as a commodity, his compliment suddenly distorted by a recollection: A week ago, the night they became engaged—the man among a group of men at an adjoining table who lurched to theirs and, staring blearily down at Gilyan, said, "You're a beauty, little girl. Like to take you home for my birthday present!" She had expected Jay to flare up with anger. Instead, he had laughed.

It was late when they reached the door of her apartment and Jay asked the unwelcome question. He had been talking about her father, Malcolm Barr, who worked out of the UPI office in London. Gilyan told him how her mother and father had bought an old house just outside Portland, Oregon, to renovate, hoping to retire there in the near future. They had been enough of traveling; Gilyan's mother had been accompanying her father since Gilyan finished school and left home, and in these two years, she had had enough of it.

After one more trip, they expected to retire. Her father wanted to do more of his freelance writing.

Jay was leaning easily against the doorframe, listening, his dark eyes sparkling with interest. "Boy! I'd give my eyeteeth or an arm for a chance at something like that!" His look alerted. "When do I get to meet your dad?"

"They have to come back fairly soon to settle things about the house. They'll return briefly to London to wind up Dad's affairs and then back for good. Why?"

Jay grasped her hand. "D'you think my future father-in-law might grease the way for me to get one of those European jobs? You'd like that, wouldn't you?"

Gilyan was angry for the sharp rejection she felt. She tried to make amends by showing interest. "Of course I would, but you're a sports reporter ... "

He shook his head impatiently. "I took the sports reporting job because I boned up on sports when there was an opening coming. I want to do a column. What I wouldn't give to get a column like The Lamplighter!" His eyes were staring into space. "I'd sure like to know how *he* got started. D'you realize he's only been writing that New York column for something under a year and is already being syndicated all over the country?"

"But Jay," Gilyan tried again, "that man's a satirist. He is obviously a writer and ... "

"And you think I'm not?" Jay's mood changed. "You think I couldn't do anything but sports?"

"Of course I don't think that! I think you could do anything you set your mind to." But even as she spoke, a needling little doubt rose deep within as to whether it was complimentary in the strictest sense. Once again, she wished she had left well enough alone.

Jay didn't seem to notice. He clasped her hands and his eyes were dancing. "Very well, then, if you think I can do anything I set my mind to, consider that I've set it to getting into something more lucrative. I'd like one of those Euroepan assignments, and if my future father-in-law takes a liking to me—who knows . . . ?"

Leaning forward, he brought his mouth down on Gilyan's and suddenly everything was all right. In his arms, she knew this was right and good. They would have a happy marriage. It was only natural that a man would like to better himself. After all, he would have a wife to think of and, loving her, to do the best he could. All was well again as they parted.

Gilyan would drive Jay to the airport Monday evening and then garage his car for him.

For most of Sunday, Gilyan had the apartment to herself and, for the first time since they had shared the apartment, she was glad that Cliff had taken Ardell out for the day. When they first got up, Ardell, seeming to sense a certain strain, tried to put it right.

The conversation took place as they ate breakfast. Ardell came to the table with a mound of golden toast and settled herself across from Gilyan, who had poached eggs and poured orange juice. Ardell's hair was soft and flyaway from the shampoo of the day before, and she was bemoaning the way it looked and handled.

"Cliff will think he's taking a wild woman to the picnic," she moaned. "My hair takes about two days of spraying before it behaves." She bit into her toast. "My hair—disgustingly enough—responds much better when it's dirty!"

Gilyan laughed. "Cliff wouldn't care if it stood straight up."

Ardell's pink cheeks deepened to the rosy color of her robe. "Isn't he a dear? You know how I'm always talking diet?" Ruefully, she eyed a second piece of toast. Ardell was inclined to stockiness and not very tall, a fact she bemoaned every time Gilyan put on one of the tailored suits so becoming to her slim height. "Cliff says," she went on, "that he likes me the way I am." She made a face. "Fat!"

"You're *not* fat," Gilyan protested.

"You're a dear, too . . . " Ardell broke off and somewhat hesitantly reached out to touch Gilyan's hand. "Gilyan, I hope I didn't upset you yesterday. I upset myself enough for two! I never should have said what I did. I was probably completely wrong, and yet I can't unsay it, can I?" The blue eyes misted. "I'm so fond of you! Cliff says I'm like a mother hen where you're concerned."

Gilyan had to laugh. "I know that. And I know you were only thinking of my welfare. You were wrong, but you meant well, and," her tone firmed, "as far as I'm concerned, it's all forgotten." If it could just be so simple. However, they finished breakfast and did the dishes in an atmosphere approximating their old intimacy.

Ardell, who was Hannah Davis's secretary, wanted to know if Gilyan thought Hannah and Roy Crofton would ever marry. Roy, a lawyer, and Hannah had been dating for several years and it was Ardell's opinion that Hannah hated the thought of giving up her work.

Gilyan wasn't so sure. "Hannah," she said, "told me that Roy was very proud of her job as Woman's Editor."

Ardell made a small *moue* of distaste. "Vida— in one of her rare moments of honoring me with her presence during a smoke in the lounge—hinted that *she* thought Hannah had carried a torch for Matt for years."

"Matt Groody?" Gilyan was startled. "Matt's very much married!"

"Of course he is. And who would listen to the viper-tongued Vida! She implied that Matt married Mrs. Groody because she owned the newspaper and that Hannah was all shook up when he married her. Honestly," Ardell wiped a plate so hard that she almost knocked it from her hand, "that Vida—a face like a Madonna and a tongue like a viper!"

Gilyan, perhaps because the newness of being in love and being loved in return made her more sensitive to the feelings of others, spoke more generously than her opinion of Vida warranted. "I think," she said slowly, "that Vida Barron is very much in love with Tom Monohan and is pretty unhappy over the fact that he never gives her a second look."

Ardell's eyes rounded. "Our Tom—the photographer? The elegant Vida in love with Tom? Good heavens! Tom loves 'em all. And he drinks too much. How did you find out?"

"Haven't you noticed how often Vida finds an excuse to go into his department? And I saw her looking after him one day as he went down the hall. It was perfectly obvious."

"Well, I'll be darned." Still trying to assimilate this news, Ardell stacked the plates on the shelf, then started when she saw the clock. "Oh—I'll never make it on time!"

Gilyan entertained Cliff until Ardell was ready. She liked the slow-spoken, slow-moving Cliff. He wasn't handsome, but he had a nice face with his freckles and crew-cut sandy hair. His eyes were as wide and clear a blue as Ardell's own. Gilyan noticed how they shone when Ardell stepped into the room. With a sigh, Gilyan knew that Ardell's and Cliff's future would be one of the very good, and lasting, ones. Then she wondered why she was sighing.

When they had left for their picnic, Gilyan threw herself into week-end chores. There were lingerie and blouses to wash and iron, the coppery hair to wash and set, and a manicure to do.

Monday evening, Gilyan dashed back to the apartment to shower and change into the slim black suit that Jay liked. Then she drove him to the airport.

They said their goodbye—their real goodbye—in the car. Holding her close, Jay put his lips against the fragrant, coppery hair looped in shiny spirals below the smart, black-feathered hat. "Ah, I'll miss you so!" He pulled back to look at her. "You'll write every day whether I get the chance to or not? You have my New York address?"

Laughing, Gilyan pulled back to smooth her hair and resettle the black feathers. "I'll write every night. Air mail. I promise. How about you?"

"I'll write every opportunity," he said, and took the key from the ignition. "Here . . . Just drop the car off at the garage. I didn't offer to let you use it while I'm gone because you have one of your own."

"Now, come on," Gilyan teased. "You didn't

offer it to me because it's shiny and new, and you're afraid I might get it dented." She was surprised to see Jay stiffen. "I'm only joking," she added.

"Well, I hope so."

At the gate, Jay clasped her hands tightly. "Don't forget, you're my girl now. As soon as I get back, we'll plan a trip up to see your folks. After all, it's important that I have the approval of my future in-laws."

Gilyan felt herself tense, and immediately hated the reaction. What was the matter with her? Of course it was important for Jay to meet her parents, and natural for him to want to do so as soon as possible. If she was going to let someone else's tentative opinion color everything Jay said the future, make her weigh his words with a balance of suspicion, then she was wronging him and herself.

In silent contrition, Gilyan put a hand to his tanned cheek. "Have a good trip, darling, and hurry back to me." Tears welled in the hazel eyes. "I'll miss you terribly."

Gilyan remained at the fence as Jay strode out and boarded the plane. She waited there for it to be airborne. The plane's engines were already revving up when she heard a babble of excitement and, from the corner of her eye, caught a bright flash of light by the gate.

Gilyan turned and saw a girl, a strikingly beautiful girl in the silken folds of a blue mink coat, a tricorn sitting smartly on silvery hair. The girl's luminous eyes were blazing in the smoothly tanned face. "Get out of my way!" she snapped. "I don't intend missing my plane for a bunch of stupid reporters!" Then one of the airline attendants had her by the arm and, amid more flashbulbs, they were running for the big silver ship.

One of the men in the group laughed, slung a camera over his shoulder and turned. It was Tom Monohan. He saw Gilyan and came toward her, grinning broadly. "Wow!" he said. "Did you get a load of the Covington dish?"

Gilyan frowned, trying to place the name. "Covington? Is she an actress?"

Tom Monohan's rugged-looking features slackened in surprise. "You didn't recognize Nancy Covington—heiress to all those beautiful millions? Gilyan, you're not up on your social notes. She's exactly twenty-five and just shed her third husband in Reno." Tom's blue eyes were on the now-moving plane. "That gal's got more money than brains. Anything Nancy sees that she wants, Nancy gets. She makes more headlines than any five actresses."

Gilyan knew why she hadn't recognized the girl, or the name. "The last picture I saw of Miss Covington, she was a decided brunette—and the newspapers usually refer to her as Minx Covington."

"And *that's* a mild nomenclature for that particular dish." Tom sounded admiring. "Did you see her take a swipe at my camera? But I was ready," he added complacently. "I got my picture."

The plane had reached the end of the runway and was air-borne in a roar of sound. Gilyan's tone was dry. "I thought Miss Covington liked publicity. From the reams accorded her, it would seem so."

"She eats it up, but I guess she cut it pretty fine making the plane, and maybe her digestion isn't so good just now. This last husband cost her a hundred thousand to shed."

Gilyan turned, and Tom fell into step with her. "Going my way?" he asked.

Gilyan waved toward the parking lot. "I have Jay's car. Do you want a ride?"

"Sure thing. I can delete taxi fare from my overburdened expense account."

Tom kept up a running line of chatter that kept Gilyan's blueness at arm's length until she dropped him off at the *Globe's* semi-darkened building.

As she parked Jay's car and climbed into her own older model, Gilyan was recalling the beautiful, petulant face of the girl in mink. Twenty-five —and three husbands. Also millions of dollars. It didn't look like those dollars could buy the girl

28

much happiness. At the rate she was going, she would be burned out at thirty. Poor Nancy Minx Covington...

Chapter Three

Gilyan had only one brief letter during the first week that Jay was gone. Disappointed, she tried to visualize how very busy he must be. The letter sounded hurried, as though he were being kept on the run.

The following Monday, Gilyan had a call from her parents, who had planed in late that afternoon. After talking to her father for five minutes, then to her mother, Gilyan found herself feeling much better. When they asked about the young man she had been mentioning in her letters so frequently, Gilyan said that Jay was in the East for a couple of weeks. However, she did tell them that she would have news for them when she saw them, and she sensed that they knew what that news would be.

For some reason, the office was bedlam on

Tuesday. Hannah was holding a sheaf of engagement announcement questionnaires when Gilyan got to work. "I think everyone in the city has been hit by Cupid's arrow at the same time!" Hannah grimaced. "You'll have to split these up with Julia. There's a big fashion show at Macklin's today and I have to cover it. Do you think you and Julia can handle these?"

Gilyan took the sheaf of questionnaires. "You don't mind if I do divide them with Julia?"

Hannah made a despairing face. "You'll have to, Sweetie. But for the love of heaven, let's proof them before Julia sends hers down. Right?"

"You know, Hannah," Gilyan said slowly, "Julia might do a lot better job of writing copy if she had more of it to do . . ."

Hannah broke in with a wave of the hand holding an unlighted cigarette and Gilyan automatically reached out to snub the smoldering cigarette in the ash tray. "I *like* Julia. I don't want to hurt her feelings, but—she just can't write! By the time you or I get through blue-penciling and editing what's she done—we've done it!" Hannah flicked the lighter to her cigarette and sat back. "These betrothal questionnaires are the only things I dare let her do. She can't go far wrong with all the facts supplied by the bride-to-be. All she has to do is fill in a few words between facts. Yet, even then," Hannah pointed her cigarette at Gilyan, "you'd better proofread them afterward."

Julia wanted so very badly to write copy. Every opera season, fashion show, Junior League event, wedding and Christmas ball, Julia's wistful looks and offers to help were hard to bypass. Hannah had softened a number of times and given Julia an assignment, then never had the heart to tell her afterward that either Hannah or Gilyan had rewritten the whole thing. Julia never appeared to sense, in reading the finished product, that very little of it was hers. In the sketching field, Julia was much better than Gilyan, but for some reason this qualification never seemed to satisfy Julia.

Hannah had straightened her maline hat and made a few strokes at her face, managing immediately to look as though she had just stepped from hours of grooming. This facility constantly amazed Gilyan. In the dark suit, with touches of frost at throat and ears, and snowy white gloves and hat, Hannah looked as though she were to be a participant in the fashion show she was covering. Her lean brown face was classic rather than beautiful, and the touches of gray in the brown hair added to this look.

Gilyan gave Julia half the questionnaire forms, and was touched to see the lovely face light up. Julia had a copy of a New York paper on her desk, turned to The Lamplighter's column. She handed it to Gilyan. "Did you read today's Lamplighter? I think he's one of the best writers in the country! His sketches on people are much wittier than they are biting. I don't see how . . . "

"Et tu?" said a deep voice, and Gilyan and Julia turned to see the tall, square form of Matt Groody. The editor of the *Globe,* a man in his forties, obviously took pride in keeping himself fit. His frosted dark hair was thick and heavy brows bristled above dark-blue eyes in the deeply tanned face. Matt's square chin jutted. "Even my own people buy a New York paper to read The Lamplighter!" he snapped. "I'd give a pretty penny to have that guy's column in my paper."

As Julia stuck the offending paper into a drawer, Gilyan told Matt she had heard from her mother and father, and his scowl disappeared. "Tell the old scoundrel to get himself down here and we'll wrestle a steak together." He turned to Julia. "I'd like to see you in my office when you have a moment."

With a wave of his hand, the big man walked out of Gilyan's office. Julia looked frightened. "What do you think he wants to see me about, Gilyan? He—he rather frightens me. You don't think I've done anything wrong?"

"Of course not. Probably wants you to do a job. Matt's a very nice person."

Julia looked a bit relieved. "You know him well, don't you?"

"He and my father are old friends. They started

out together as club reporters for the old *Oregonian*."

Ardell called from the hall door: "I just made some coffee if anyone's interested."

Looking worried again, Julia shook her head and went down the hall toward Matt's office as Gilyan followed Ardell into the small lounge the girls had managed to make less bleak than the storeroom it had originally been. Ardell was washing printer's ink from her hands. "The files," she said, "seem to be in their own private uproar this morning. Hannah has me looking up a bunch of stuff on the past opera season, and I'm a mess." The usually sunny face of her roommate looked hot and cross.

They sat down at the table with cups of coffee. "Where'd my slave-driving boss go?" Ardell asked, tentatively touching her tongue to the hot coffee. "Careful," she gasped. "The lava's fresh from the crater."

"Hannah had to cover a fashion show at Macklin's. She says we're swamped, that Cupid must have hit every couple in town at the same time. I'm going to have to make this coffee break a quick one."

"Speaking of Cupid," Ardell said easily, "did you get a letter this morning? The mail hadn't come when I left." She managed a sip of coffee. "Those blasted files were why I dashed off so early."

Gilyan shook her head. "Nope. But Jay said he was afraid he couldn't get too much time to write."

Ardell made it easier for Gilyan. "When they're covering a series, you can bet your sweet life it keeps them hopping. You'll probably hear tomorrow. Oh—oh . . . " The last was *sotto voce,* and Gilyan looked up to see Vida Barron gliding into the room.

Vida's looks were dramatic—black hair and light, greenish-blue eyes, and a complexion that was the envy of cosmeticians. Where Julia Caldwell's beauty was done in pastels, nature had brushed this girl in bold strokes of color. Vida, unfortunately, was completely aware of her striking looks. Yet, it wasn't only that, Gilyan considered. There was a coldness about the girl, a streak of something bordering on unfeelingness that kept others from feeling close to her, or wanting to be. Added to this, Vida had the disconcerting habit of saying exactly what she thought. She proceeded to do so now.

"It must be nice," her tone was languid, "to be at work for less than an hour and be able to stop for coffee."

"What are *you* doing in here?" Ardell snapped.

"I've been working since nine," Vida said smoothly. "I saw Gilyan come in after ten, and now," she lifted a white wrist, "it is exactly two minutes to eleven."

"It so happens that Gilyan," Gilyan said levelly, "spent the hour from nine to almost ten at the Breakfast Club covering a speaker. I'm surprised you're so interested in my comings and goings, Vida. Are you acting as our official time clock?" She couldn't resist it. "Better watch it—time clocks get punched." Immediately, she felt ashamed of herself. What was the matter with everyone this morning? Hannah upset, Matt angry about not having a Lamplighter on his staff, Julia frightened, Ardell crossly overworked, and now a barb from Vida.

Ardell gave a whoop of laughter, and Vida spun on her. "What's so funny?"

"*You!*" Ardell said, still laughing. "You don't often get back what you dish out. And particularly not from Gilyan, who's too polite for her own good."

Vida sniffed. "Frankly, I prefer her outspokenness to some other traits she has!"

Surprised, Gilyan stared at the dark-haired girl. "Naturally, I won't disappoint you by not asking what you mean." She saw that Vida's hand was shaking as she lighted a cigarette. The look she turned on Gilyan was icy.

"Oh, come on," Vida drawled. "I thought you were late this morning due to the many romances you have simmering on the same fire."

Ardell's round blue eyes widened. Gilyan finally managed, "You can be clearer than that, Vida. You are usually much more to the point."

"Very well." An orange-tipped finger deliberately snubbed out the newly lighted cigarette and Vida looked up, the blue-green eyes narrowed. "It just seems to me that when you're at the airport tenderly seeing one man off, it's a little risky having another one there to meet you, isn't it?"

So that was it. Vida had found out about Tom riding back to the office with her. Tom had probably told her so himself. If Gilyan wasn't so full of disappointment because Jay hadn't written again, she would have felt sorry for Vida. As it was, she snapped, "Don't be ridiculous, Vida! I'm not even remotely interested in Tom Monohan."

"Oh, no!" Ardell exclaimed, and was again laughing helplessly. Vida turned on her heel and left the room.

Ardell wiped her mirth-filled eyes. "You were right, Gilyan. She is in love with Tom. But," Ardell's voice turned serious, "if I were you—I'd watch Vida. She's the type that's determined to get back at someone whether they've actually done anything to her or not."

Gilyan made a small *moue* of distaste. "Vida Barron doesn't bother me . . . " And almost added, "The only thing bothering me is not hearing from Jay." Fortunately, she bit it back in time. Before their recent conversation about Jay, she could have told Ardell how upset she was at having only one letter, and Ardell would have sympathized with her, told her that of course everything was all right, that Jay was busy. Now, Gilyan couldn't even have the solace of seeking Ardell's sympathetic ear.

Moodily, Gilyan returned to her office. Her conscience smote her as she saw Julia, who had worriedly gone to see Matt, and realized that she hadn't given the girl another thought. She walked into the next small office off her own and crossed to Julia's desk.

"Julia, is everything all right?"

Startled, the amber eyes came up and Gilyan saw that the slender blonde girl had been busy on her half of the questionnaires. Again, Gilyan was touched. If she could just help Julia with her writing. This, however, posed a problem. Julia always went directly home from work and she never asked anyone over to her place. The amber eyes were clear and serene. A smile twinkled up at Gilyan. "I was frightened for nothing," Julia said in her soft, light-girl voice. "Mr. Groody just told me that when Ardell gets swamped on the filing, I'm to help her."

Gilyan perched for a moment on Julia's desk. "I love your dress," she said. The silvery-blue wool sheer was beautifully cut.

Julia looked down, smoothing the rich wool. "Isn't it gorgeous? The one cousin is just my size.

I don't have to take in a tuck, or change a hemline. I'm lucky."

Gilyan smiled and headed back into her own office. The matter of clothing seemed little enough luck for poor Julia. She had a number of well-to-do cousins in the East who sent her their cast-off clothes. Julia, thanks to the cousins, dressed beautifully, no small blessing with her unimpressive salary and an invalid aunt to care for. Gilyan's own pay would have been hard pressed, too, if it weren't for her parents frequently buying materials from England and Scotland that her mother had made up for her. Working on the Woman's Page of a big city daily meant going to social affairs, meeting celebrities, and covering the opera, plus countless other events. Gilyan sent a silent blessing to Julia's Eastern cousin and hoped they didn't change their bountiful habits.

Monday and Tuesday passed with no word from Jay, and Gilyan noticed that when Ardell came in from work Tuesday night, she pointedly didn't ask whether Gilyan had heard. After this length of time, she must know that Gilyan was upset. Yet nothing was said. Ominous? If there had been any kind of an accident, she would have heard. It was simply that Jay was a poor correspondent. Many people were, newspaper people notoriously so.

Ardell and Cliff were going to a show and both

of them asked Gilyan to join them, but Gilyan smilingly rejected the offer by saying she had too many things to do and, after they left, wished this were true.

Reading or watching television didn't help. The words she read were no better than meaningless stretches of the alphabet spinning across white magazine pages and the television a series of sounds. About nine o'clock, she tried to call her parents, then was relieved when the operator said there was no answer. They might have sensed her upset. And not having met Jay, this could give them an erroneous impression of him. When the operator asked if she would like her to try the number again, Gilyan canceled the call. Jay, at this very moment, might be trying to reach her.

Gilyan showered with the bathroom door open in order to hear the telephone, then slipped into a long jade wool robe piped in satin and again tried to read. It was no good. What could possibly take all of Jay's time? If she were away, Gilyan could conceive of no situation being so time consuming that she wouldn't at least snatch fifteen minutes in which to write a few lines to Jay. Naturally, he was busy, but not possibly that busy. And his one letter had been a hurried, impersonal thing.

Gilyan felt her eyes fill and angrily got to her feet. She creamed her face, brushed the shining coppery hair, and determinedly climbed into bed with a new book. She had closed her bedroom door, and when she heard Ardell's subdued entrance into the living room, she quickly switched out the reading light. She heard Ardell showering and stirring around in her bedroom, but sleep didn't come until much later.

Wednesday morning, there was no letter from Jay, and Gilyn went to work with what felt like a permanent lump in her throat.

Just before noon, Hannah stuck her head into Gilyan's office. She had the inevitable cigarette in one hand and a hairbrush in the other. "Gilyan, I have a stubborn patch of hair on the back of my head. Will you smooth it down?" Her look sharpened. "Are you feeling under the weather?"

Gilyan rose, shaking her head. "No. I've just been busy on these engagement forms." She picked up a piece of tissue and wiped her hands. "I'm almost finished with this batch, thank heaven."

"Oh." To Gilyan's relief, Hannah accepted her explanation. "Let's go into what we laughingly call our lounge, and if you'll brush this mop down, maybe I can get my hat on." Hannah sighed as they walked down the hall and into the converted storeroom. "Sometimes I think if I have to cover another luncheon and listen to another speaker, I'll scream." She sat down before the mirror.

Gilyan took the brush and lightly brought it

over the surface of Hannah's hair.

Ardell walked in with Julia. "We have an announcement of note." She sounded bitter. "Julia and I have *almost* conquered the files."

Hannah was somewhat gingerly setting the cluster of roses comprising her hat onto her bouffed hair. When she turned around, she was, as usual, a picture of the smartly groomed woman.

Gilyan shook her head. "I don't know how you do it, Hannah. You always look like something out of *Vogue*, the moment you stop working."

Hannah hooted. "Look who's talking! Don't you *know* why I always cover the debs' affairs and let you handle the social doings of the senior citizens? Because every time one of those Junior Leaguers or debs see you they turn pale green! Then they grow a chip on their shoulder toward the press . . . "

"Speaking of turning green . . . " Vida was standing in the doorway. The moment Gilyan saw her pale, composed face with the vivid red mouth parted in a smile that didn't reach the blue-green eyes, she felt a flash of fear. Evidently, the others in the room felt some intangible, too, for Vida had everyone's full attention and she stood there in the doorway, savoring it, before going on. Her eyes were intent on Gilyan.

"Haven't you heard the news?" The words were slow. "Why no, of course you haven't. It just came over the wire services. Jay Hanover and Nancy-

Minx Covington eloped last night. Their short courtship started on the plane where they first met—en route to New York."

Chapter Four

High over a mauve bank of swirling clouds, Gilyan stared unseeingly at a silver wing of the plane. Even the motors didn't penetrate the merciful numbness still gripping her.

Had it been today, only a few hours ago, that Vida Barron had walked into the lounge and told Gilyan about Jay?

Vaguely, she knew sharp words had been hurled at Vida from Ardell and Hannah. And she fuzzily recalled Hannah making her lie back on the old chaise while Ardell went flying for Gilyan's coat; she remembered shivering with a terrible coldness. Firmly, Ardell and Hannah had taken matters into their own hands. They had Julia call the airlines for a round-trip reservation to Portland, and then Hannah had seen Matt Groody. Ardell and Hannah packed for Gilyan and took her to the plane. Gilyan dimly recalled Hannah's telling her, as she boarded the big jet, that she wasn't to come back to the paper until the following Monday; not then, if she didn't feel up to it.

Apparently, one of the girls called her parents for when the plane came to rest at the Oregon airfield, the first person Gilyan saw was her father. The concerned gray eyes as the tall figure moved through the crowd toward her suddenly melted the ice around Gilyan and, putting out her hands to him, the tears started. Wordlessly, his arms went around her and Gilyan felt as she had when she was small and Mother or Dad's presence always made the hurt lessen. Just as they could, by their understanding and sympathy, make seemingly gigantic problems diminish in size.

"Come on, Baby," her father said, clearing his throat. "The car's over here."

Ducking her head against his arm, trying desperately to hold back the sobs hurting her throat, Gilyan blindly followed him. Her mother, a slim, older edition of Gilyan, was standing by the car and came forward to put her arms around her daughter. It was as though a death had occurred and loved ones rallied around. And, actually, it had been a death. The death of Jay's love for her, of her hopes for a lifetime by his side. Gilyan clung tightly to her mother for a moment, then climbed into the car.

She looked at her father, then at her mother.

45

"You—you both look so wonderful to me!" she said.

Karen Barr's hazel eyes, set in a fringe of heavy black so like her daughter's, were troubled above the smiling mouth. "It seems like years since we've seen you, honey." Firmly, she tucked one of Gilyan's hands into hers as Malcolm Barr turned the big car onto the freeway.

"You," her mother said, "may talk when we get home. Right now, it's your father's and my turn. We've reams of London reports!"

Gilyan leaned back and listened to the two people dear to her, appreciating their thoughtful diplomacy. They had always been this way. Since her youngest days, Gilyan never recalled anything but consideration from either of them. It was never an unequivocal No, you can't do this or must do that! It was always a discussion as to why she should—or should not. And Gilyan never recalled a time when they hadn't said, Thank you, or Please.

It was late evening before Gilyan felt that she could talk. They were sitting in the living room of their city apartment, a fire crackling on the hearth, fresh coffee on the small table between the fire and the couch. Gilyan set down her coffee cup and looked over at her father in the big blue chair to the right of the fireplace, then to her mother sitting beside her on the divan.

"I—I want to thank you both for the way

46

you've helped today. I—I don't think I could have borne it if you'd still been over in London." Then, clearing her throat, speaking almost without expression, Gilyan told them about Jay. Told them how Jay had asked her to marry him on his return from New York. Told them how she had taken him to the plane and had seen Nancy Covington boarding right afterward. How she had had only one letter from him, and how the news had come over the wire services and been relayed to her. She skipped Vida; her cattishness and obvious relish in relaying the news to Gilyan were superficial. But Ardell's doubts were dealt with as just that; doubts. Her own doubts, fears, when she didn't hear from Jay, but never once fearing the thing that did happen. Her fear wasn't of another girl; her fear had been that Jay, away from her, wasn't as interested as when he was by her side.

When Gilyan had finished, she looked up. Her father's face wouldn't have said much except for the white ring around his mouth. That ring didn't appear often, but when it did, he was deeply, thoroughly angry. However, his voice, when he spoke, was controlled.

"And you say Ardell was a little withdrawn about Hanover?"

"Yes."

"Anything specific?"

"Not really, Dad. She thought him an opportunist."

"Looks like she might have been right."

Gilyan didn't speak, and her mother turned to look at her daugher. "I wouldn't dare tell you how bad I feel for you. If I did, the dam would burst." She reached out a hand. "Actually, in a case like this, there's nothing anyone can say in the initial stages to lessen the hurt. Only one thing can do that for you—time. I know this doesn't sound possible at this moment, but believe me, darling, it's true. I think," she sent a warning look toward Gilyan's father, "it would be in error for us to say anything right now because of the way we feel. We're both very angry, hurt to see the way you've been hurt. We'll wait a few days—at least you'll be here a day or so longer—until Malc and I have cooled down, somewhat; then we'll talk about it."

Malcolm Barr gave a sharp bark of laughter. "Your mother's so right, Baby. My discussion right now would be on a completely emotional level and would most likely consist of some pretty blue-hued words. In fact, I can't think of any other kind at the moment."

As Gilyan lay sleepless in her bed some hours later, she understood her father's deep anger; also, her mother's. But Gilyan herself hadn't reached the stage of revivifying anger or aroused pride. Her feeling was a sick gnawing that made her close her eyes in sheer pain whenever she thought of the girl she had seen by the airport gate, in Jay's arms, wearing Jay's ring, his name.

Suddenly, Gilyan knew that her mother was in the room. There had been no sound, just a faint wafting of the familiar perfume she always associated with her mother. "Mother . . . ?"

"Yes, dear." The voice came softly from the bedside. "I didn't want to make a sound in case you were asleep. In case you weren't—here."

The little bed lamp clicked on and her mother extended a pill and a glass of water. "I don't advocate making sedatives a habit, but tonight you have one."

Gratefully, Gilyan took the small pink pill and washed it down with water. "Thanks, Mother."

Her mother swept the froth of creamy lace of her peignoir to one side and settled lightly on the edge of the bed. "Shall we have a gabfest while you're getting to sleep?"

Gilyan nodded. "Like old times." Impulsively, she took her mother's hand, touching the almond-shaped, rose-tinted nails. "I'm so glad you and Dad are going to stay in Oregon. It always gives me a hollow feeling when you're so far off."

The hazel eyes softened in the downbent face so like Gilyan's. "Well, now," she said, "I *think* you might've had a bit to do with our decision to retire early. We weren't exactly enthusiastic about having an ocean between us." The red mouth parted over white teeth. "Of course Malc wants more time for his article writing, too—so don't let all this turn your head, young lady!"

"I don't care about all the reasons—just the results." Gilyan's lids were becoming heavy. "Talk some more, Mother."

"Oh, I intend to. We brought you something rather extra special this time. I think you're going to . . . " Gilyan's heavily fringed lids flew wide open. "Oh, oh! Wrong subject!" Her mother smiled. "Now close your eyes and I'll be boring." She saw the creamy lids droop. "We're going to take you out to see the house while you're here. It's coming along beautifully. The floors have to be laid in the living room and the guest bathroom and bedroom have to . . . " Her voice tapered off and her face was compassionate as she looked down on her sleeping daughter's face, so young and vulnerable looking in sleep.

On Sunday, a few hours before Gilyan had to take the plane, Gilyan and her mother sat in the white brick kitchen drinking coffee. There were new hollows in Gilyan's cheeks and umber streaks under the hazel eyes, but the days with her parents had helped. They had neither lectured her nor condemned Jay. They had tried, instead, to show her that a worse tragedy would have occurred if Jay hadn't gone East, if he and Gilyan had married in haste. It was obvious that Jay Hanover was mentally immature and a greater tragedy would have resulted if their marriage had taken place and then his feelings toward her had changed. At first, Gilyan rather feebly tried to take the stand that perhaps if they had married, Jay wouldn't have changed. But even as she advanced this theory, she realized that it was a weak one. A mentally mature person would not have committed himself to loving one girl in one week and marrying another the next.

Gilyan set down her coffee cup. "I'm glad it's so cool. I can wear my new mink stole. Do you and Dad know how much I adore it?"

Her mother smiled. "We had a feeling you would. It will go beautifully with your beige suit."

Gilyan remembered something she had been intending to ask her mother. "Do you or Dad ever hear from Rob Hunter?"

Her mother rose to get fresh coffee, and she spoke over her shoulder. "Rob's in the East." She turned. "More coffee?"

Gilyan shook her head. "Doing what?"

"I'm not exactly sure."

"That's funny. I asked Dad the other night, and he was vague, too. I rather thought Rob would always keep in touch with you and Dad." Gilyan smiled. "Sometimes I don't think he had nearly the crush on *me* he thought he had. I think it was you and Dad who held the most attraction. I think half the time he came to the house to visit you folks. He could talk writing to you and Dad for hours."

"I wouldn't say that," her mother said mildly, coming back to the table.

"Mother," Gil's tone was serious, "I've always

wanted to say this to you, and now is a good opportunity. I know what a fine person Rob is and how disappointed you both were when I couldn't seem to return his love. Yet neither of you have ever scolded, and"—her voice thickened—"during this bad time you've never once intimated an I-told-you-so attitude."

"Now, listen." Her mother's tone was brisk. "That's nonsense. Of course we like Rob. Of course we hoped you'd come to care for him. But we also knew it wasn't your fault if you didn't. Love—to cite an old cliche—isn't some tap labeled hot or cold, to be turned on or off at will! Rob understood that, too."

As Gilyan replied, she subconsciously noted that her mother was still evading her original question. She doubted very much that Rob hadn't kept in touch with them. They probably knew exactly where he was and what he was doing and, for some reason—Gilyan rather got the idea that Rob must have another girl—they didn't want to volunteer this information. She wished she could tell them that it wouldn't bother her, but she didn't know exactly how to phrase it without sounding unfeeling. Instead, she followed her mother's thought about her not having returned Rob's feeling.

"I think perhaps it was because Rob was always there. In high school and college, I mean. I loved him, but as a brother. I always knew what a fine person he was, but Rob always seemed so—well, so rather pacific. A dreamer. Not a very sophisticated person, really."

"Is sophistication so important?" her mother asked in the same mild tone.

"Well, I think so," Gilyan said. "You and Dad are certainly sophisticates—in a very nice way."

"We're also a couple of decades-plus older than Rob. We didn't acquire it in young adulthood."

Malcolm Barr walked into the kitchen. "What are we having? A bull session?"

"We were just talking about Rob Hunter," Gilyan said. "I asked Mother what he's doing now."

"He's in the East," her father said, the term beginning to sound a bit repetitive, as he poured himself a cup of coffee.

Gilyan was convinced that Rob must be engaged or married, the way they were acting. Her only reaction was the hope that it would be to someone as nice as Rob.

Malcolm Barr sat down with his coffee. "How's Matt?" he asked. "Is Rigley working out at the City Desk?"

"I guess so. You'd be surprised how little we on the Woman's Page see of the people in the editorial office; how little contact we have with Jim Rigley. Matt wanders in once in a while. And, by the way, he said to tell you he hopes to see you soon. I think his expression was that he wanted to wrestle a steak with you."

Malcolm laughed. "How's Alice?" He shook his head. "I haven't seen either of them for almost two years."

"She's fine, I guess. I had lunch with her about six months ago, but other than that, I only see her when she comes into the office." Gilyan felt more relaxed than she had at any time since coming home. It was good to be on an impersonal subject. "One of the girls in our office, Julia Caldwell, is scared to death of Matt. He came in the other day and did some barking, then asked to see her—and she was terribly frightened. Her job's important to her."

Malcolm's eyes twinkled. "Is she pretty?"

Surprised, Gilyan looked up. "Julia? Yes, lovely. Why?"

Her father laughed. "I was just thinking of the old Matt. Fifteen years ago, he wouldn't have frightened a pretty girl over his bark—or her job."

"Why?"

Malcolm Barr sobered. "Actually, I guess it wasn't too funny, but when Matt was younger, he had a weakness for girls. Anyone with a pretty face could send him into a tailspin."

Gilyan was astonished. *"Matt Groody?"*

"Yep. In fact, he lost more than one job over this weakness. A couple of his bosses had good-looking wives, and Matt was a handsome young buck."

"He's still a good-looking man." Gilyan's sur-

54

prise was intense. Matt never, by word or look, showed any interest in the girls around the newspaper office, and he had some good-looking ones working there. Vida . . . Gilyan swiftly shut off thought of Vida. Julia. Hannah was older, but still a very good-looking woman.

Karen noticed Gilyan's look. "He's changed, Gilyan. He's been behaving himself for years. Outgrew his pranks a long time ago. I think he and Alice have a good marriage."

"One of the girls said something to Ardell," Gilyan said slowly. "Something to the effect that it was rumored Matt married Alice because of her money. Because she owned the *Globe*."

"Nonsense!" Malcolm snorted. "I told you Matt's weakness—when he was younger—was females, not money. Matt's put a lot into that paper and made money for Alice. Anyway, as your mother said, theirs seems a good marriage."

"You still gave me a jolt," Gilyan said. "Somehow, Matt's so brusque and businesslike, I can't visualize him in the role of a Lothario."

Her father looked at the copper wall clock and changed the subject. "Where's Belle? Isn't she working today?"

Karen Barr shook her head. "I had her fix us a cold supper and go. Her sister's expecting a baby —her first—and Belle's been working here, with her mind there." She, too, looked up at the clock. "I guess we'd better get it on, Gilyan. Your plane

55

will be leaving in a couple of hours." She sighed. "I wish you could have stayed longer."

"She's promised to come up here on her vacation when we get back," Malcolm Barr said. "We'll look forward to that."

Gilyan held tightly to each parent just before boarding the plane, her eyes threatening to overflow. "I—I don't know what I should have done without you," she said. "The awful hurt's still here, but I can bear it now."

Karen's eyes misted and Malcolm suddenly and violently cleared his throat, then saved the threatening moment of emotion by holding Gilyan off and saying, "Baby, you ought to wear those tawny tones all the time. They do something with that coppery hair." He looked at her mother. "With no hint of smugness, I'd say I have the two best-looking women in the state on my arm."

"We sure are," Karen said complacently.

"Frankly, I think the mink stole has a bit to do with it." Gilyan picked up the light thread.

Karen turned to her daughter. "Really, that wasn't a very smart remark. We'd be beautiful in sackcloth and ashes!" She leaned forward. "At least your father thinks so. Don't disabuse him, poor thing!"

Gilyan left them, smiling.

Chapter Five

Cliff and Ardell met Gilyan's plane, and Ardell set the tone for what could have been a bad moment by exclaiming over Gilyan's new furs. Neither she nor Cliff, on the ride from the airport to the apartment, said a word about Jay. Gilyan was grateful for that.

On Monday, Hannah, whether by accident or design, launched Gilyan into a schedule that was busy enough for two people. Julia, off with a bad cold, still wasn't in by Wednesday, and Gilyan, during one of the few moments she had free, called Ardell into the lounge to ask what they should do about seeing if Julia was all right or needed anything.

Ardell scowled. "Hannah and I were talking about it, too," she said. "But we don't think Julia would appreciate anyone coming around. I don't know whether her aunt is a tartar, or whether Julia's ashamed of the place where they live. Perhaps it's a combination of both. However, she never asks anyone over. Remember when we had that shower at the apartment for Cecily and Julia wanted to donate the cake because, she said, she couldn't ever return an invitation or give a shower herself?"

Gilyan nodded. "Yes, I know. But it doesn't seem right to wait until Julia gets back to work to find out how she is. And she has no telephone in the apartment proper because it disturbs her aunt —she says. Frankly, I think poor little Julia can't afford a telephone. We can't call the one in the hall when we don't know the apartment listing."

Ardell grimaced. "Perhaps we could send something over to her with a note?"

Gilyan nodded. "Yes. And tell her in the note to call us if she wants anything, that we're all concerned."

Gilyan found it good to be worrying about someone else. Since getting back into the stride of her work, she had discovered the annoying facility on her part of being able to do the work with half her mind, leaving the other half to dwell on the grief and hurt that seemed to fill her body with an aching void.

"I'll leave early on my lunch hour." Ardell finished her coffee and rose. "Shall I get flowers or fruit?" She outlined her mouth with a pale pink lipstick. "What shall I say on the card?"

"Are you going anywhere near Union Square?" Gilyan asked.

"I can go there as easily as anywhere else. Why?"

"I was just thinking that perhaps it would give Julia more of a lift if we got her some little luxury bauble that she couldn't afford for herself. A pin—or a bracelet?"

Doubtfully, Ardell nodded. "Perhaps," she said slowly. "But those cousins keep Julia so exquisitely dressed, I'm almost afraid to pick out an accessory. And come to think of it, they must also supply the costume jewelry she wears. Have you noticed how good looking the few pieces are that she does wear?"

Gilyan made a face. "You're right, of course. Could we send her one of those attractive fruit packs?"

"I think that would be better. About ten dollars, you think?"

Gilyan nodded and picked up her alligator bag and pulled out a five and a one. "There'll be a tax to split, too," she said. "Just write on the note that we're worried about her and didn't know exactly how to offer our services in case she might need them."

"It just doesn't seem right—" Ardell started. "Julia's so sweet and pretty, yet she hasn't a single

59

boy friend . . . " Ardell broke off and Gilyan looked at her levelly. This was no good. Things between them must not be permitted to deteriorate to the point where certain subjects must be avoided.

Gilyan's tone was even. "I've wondered about that myself," she said. "With Julia's looks, you'd think she'd be surrounded by boy friends."

Ardell looked relieved. "But she isn't, Gilyan! In fact, from the little she says of her home life, she seldom dates. Most evenings are spent with her aunt. Well," Ardell tucked Gilyan's money into her purse, "I'll dash."

Gilyan moved over to the wall mirror to smooth the coppery hair, then took out her lipstick. It was as she moved the vivid orange cylinder across her mouth that she saw Vida behind her, reflected in the mirror. Gilyan's hand jerked, and she bent forward with a piece of tissue to rub away the crooked line. Vida threw her verbal blockbuster.

"Gilyan, I want to apologize to you for being so bitchy the other day. I'm sorry for the way I told you the news, and I'm sorry about what Jay Hanover did to you."

For a long moment, Gilyan didn't know what to say. Then she turned and looked at the blue-green eyes staring back at her. Was there malice in them? No. There actually seemed to be an expression of concern. Gilyan swallowed. "I—won't say it wasn't the hard way to find out."

The smooth black head shook slowly from side to side. "From my own viewpoint," Vida said distinctly, "I would find it inexcusable. If someone did to me what I did to you, I'd most likely pull some of their hair out. But then," she added simply, "I'm not a very nice person."

Gilyan was torn in two directions. She wanted to tell Vida that she didn't think she was a very nice person, either, that most of their fellow workers shared this opinion. On the other hand, her badly bruised emotions were touched by the obviously sincere attempt to apologize by someone who wouldn't ordinarily do so. Gilyan blurted the first thing that came to mind. "Why—I mean, why aren't you—as you say—a very nice person?"

Vida's expression didn't change. "I couldn't possibly bore you with the many factors that have gone into producing the end result that is me—Vida Barron—a not-very-nice person. Perhaps the latest contributing factor, you deserve to be told. You know how I feel about Tom Monohan, of course. Perhaps my bitterness is increased because he not only doesn't return my feeling, but likes someone else who doesn't return his. He's drinking more than is good for him and endangering what could be an excellent career."

Gilyan was shocked to see tears well up in the blue-green eyes. Vida didn't lift a hand to wipe them away. Gilyan sought something to say, and

61

again blurted out the first thing that came into her mind.

"I'm sorry. Who—who is Tom in love with?"

"Julia Caldwell," Vida said quietly.

"Julia!" Gilyan gasped. "Why she doesn't . . . " She bit back the rest of the phrase, but Vida finished it for her.

"Doesn't know Tom's alive?" Vida nodded, mechanically raising a hand to her face and brushing the tears aside. "Tom's been eating his heart out for Julia since shortly after she came to work here. He comes to my place and tells me how lovely, how sweet, she is. I'm" the red mouth twisted, "his sounding board! His crying towel."

To Gilyan's relief, Hannah's heels clicked to the doorway and Vida brushed past Gilyan to the inner dressing room.

Hannah dropped onto the lounge and lit a cigarette. "Matt's walking on air," she said, and it surprised Gilyan that Hannah didn't notice the supercharged atmosphere. To her, the room seemed to be echoing with Vida's surprising statements. She pulled her mind back to what Hannah was saying. "He says he thinks he can work a deal to carry The Lamplighter's column."

"Oh . . . ?" Gilyan turned back to the mirror. "Will his column appeal to San Franciscans?"

Hannah looked surprised. "Of course. He does his profiles on people who are well known from coast to coast." Her look sharpened. "Things pretty grim, Gilyan?" she asked hesitantly.

Gilyan's mouth shook, and she firmed it. Sympathy was devastating to her. "Grim enough," she said.

"Gilyan," Hannah lowered her voice, "I'll have something to tell you in the near future. Something about our work," she added hastily as Vida walked out of the dressing room, her face once again smooth and remote. Hannah stared at her until she had left the lounge. "I didn't know anyone was in there! I'm glad I didn't go on. Especially with Vida. When I tell you, it's for your ears alone."

Ordinarily, Gilyan's curiosity would have been whetted, but right now she found it difficult even to show the expected polite interest. "I'll be looking forward to hearing what it is," she said.

Hannah got up. "Well, I'm off. Mrs. Darlinger's favorite niece is throwing an engagement party tonight, and when Mrs. Darlinger beckons, we respond. If she withdraws her support—as rumored —of the opera next season, San Francisco's going to be in trouble." Gilyan didn't realize until later that this information had registered on her mind.

Late that afternoon, Julia called, her voice a croak, to thank Gilyan and Ardell for the basket of fruit. Gilyan scolded her for being out of bed. "You mean you came out into the hall to call us?

63

Julia, you shouldn't have! Is there anything we can do?"

Julia hastily assured her there wasn't and promised to get right back to bed.

Saturday night, Ardell and Cliff insisted that Gilyan accompany them to a party—a reunion of Cliff's college fraternity. It was to be a large affair and a dozen extra guests could walk in without upsetting the elastic arrangements. Gilyan, already in her green robe, started to demur, then realized that another long evening alone was to be avoided at all costs. If she read a book, watched television, or listened to music on the radio, some part of the plot, some characterization or tune always recalled Jay with a flash of pain.

"If you'll wait until I change," she surprised Ardell by saying, "I'll enjoy going very much."

Gilyan chose a heavy white silk, tightly fitting through the bodice and the skirt softly draped across her slim hips. She wore chunky gold and chalky, fresh-water pearls with it. And a full taffeta coat of emerald green that highlighted the coppery hair. Cliff whistled as she walked back into the living room.

"That'll be enough of that," Ardell said with mock severity. "I really don't know why I asked such a decorative wench."

At the big hotel, Gilyan found the babble of voices, the endless introductions to people she was quite likely never to meet again, the clink of ice in glasses, laughter and music, to be exactly what she needed. Completely impersonal and superficial. "How are you, Miss Barr? It's been nice meeting you." There were compliments and bold flattery, and several of Cliff's friends attempted to flirt with her as they danced and tried to make dates, but Gilyan just smiled and turned them down. But it was all healing.

Late in the evening, feeling welcomely tired and hoping Cliff and Ardell would soon want to leave, she had excused herself from a group to find Ardell, when a man, whose name Gilyan had since forgotten, touched her arm. He was with another young man, a tall, rather slightly built, dark-haired man with expressive dark eyes. It was odd, a corner of her mind noted, that a man built like Jay and with very much his coloring, could actually be so dissimilar. The first man was speaking.

"Miss Barr, a friend of mine—late in arriving—wants to meet you. Miss Barr—Phil Randall—Dr. Randall."

Gilyan murmured something and Dr. Randall asked if she would care to dance. Gilyan laughed ruefully. "I'm sorry, Dr. Randall, but I'm very tired."

The expressive dark eyes showed instant concern. "May I get you a drink? Would you like to go out onto the balcony and rest your feet? I can bring you something out there."

Gilyan didn't see Cliff or Ardell, so she nodded.

Dr. Randall had attended medical school in the East, then come to San Francisco to go into practice. From the way he talked, he was doing well. He told Gilyan that he had been tired and almost didn't come to the reunion, but now he was glad he had.

Firmly, Gilyan led the conversation into impersonal channels. From his olive complexion and expressive dark eyes, she thought Dr. Randall might be of Latin extraction, and she was surprised to learn that he was Scotch. He amused her with some Scottish anecdotes and Gilyan was laughing when Cliff and Ardell appeared in the balcony doorway.

Gilyan introduced them to the doctor, then told Ardell she was ready to go home.

"If your friends would rather stay," Dr. Randall suggested, "I can drive you home."

Gilyan gave Ardell a look that was clearer than a headshake.

"Thank you, Doctor, but we were ready to leave." Ardell sounded reluctant.

"May I call you sometime, Miss Barr?" Dr. Randall asked Gilyan as they walked inside for their wraps.

Gilyan didn't know what to say. She didn't want to hurt him, yet she hadn't the slightest desire to encourange him. She just wasn't interested. She was spared answering as a white-coated waiter touched Dr. Randall's sleeve. "You're wanted on the telephone, sir. The call from the hospital you were expecting."

"Oh . . . Excuse me. I won't be long."

Gilyan refused to wait. "I only met the man less than an hour ago, Ardell. Why should I wait while a perfect stranger finishes his telephone call? Please do come along."

"Okay." Ardell shrugged. "You know best." And then, as though afraid she sounded disapproving, Ardell took Gilyan's arm and pressed it as they walked out of the Terrace Room and to the elevator.

In the car, Cliff gave a rending yawn. "I'm stunned with the need for sleep," he said. "Did you tell Gilyan our news?"

"Oh, Cliff!" Ardell wailed. "If that isn't just like a man!"

"But I *am* a man," Cliff said. "What's wrong?"

"I wanted to tell Gilyan tonight, when we were alone."

Cliff sounded genuinely puzzled. "I'll never understand the feminine mind. The news is definitely half mine, but I'm not supposed to be around when it's told."

Gilyan laughed at his tone. "Shame on you, Ardell, keeping Cliff out of his own news. Now, what is it?"

In the light of the dash, Ardell's look was half-happy, half-worried. Gilyan suddenly knew what was coming. "Cliff and I have decided that if Uncle Sam hasn't called Cliff by the end of October, we'll plan to be married sometime during November."

Gilyan turned to the girl on the seat beside her and hugged her. "Oh, Ardell, I'm so very happy for you!" She refused to acknowledge the sharp pang deep within her.

"No wonder you wanted to tell her when you were alone!" Cliff sounded offended. "Nobody acts like I'm here, or have anything to do with this happy event!"

Gilyan leaned forward in the seat and blew Cliff a kiss. "Now why do you think I'm so happy for Ardell, you big goose? Because she got *you*, that's why!"

A board grin flexed Cliff's mouth. "Ah, that fixes it. You said *exactly* the right thing, my good young woman."

Later, in their apartment, Gilyan had to laugh as she was creaming her face and brushing her hair. Ardell kept popping in and out of the room like a jack-in-the-box. She was full of a thousand and one happy details. It was as though walls had fallen now that she found she could tell Gilyan about the wedding without, apparently, hurting her. In the face of her roommate's happiness, Gilyan entered into the spirit of the plans and hid all trace of pain, any of the ache she felt about an approaching wedding date that could very well have been her own.

Gilyan, finally in bed, heard Ardell approaching for what seemed the hundredth time and once again flicked on the light to smile up at her friend.

"I forgot to tell you." Ardell's voice sounded timid, as though Gilyan might scold. "The doctor you met tonight. I—I think he really liked you, Gilyan. Why didn't you want him to have your telephone number? He seemed such a nice person."

Gilyan shook her head. "It's just too soon, Ardell. I'll date again—I hope—but not right now."

Ardell's face puckered like that of a small girl. "Oh, Gilyan, I've been selfish tonight, rattling on about our plans."

Gilyan put out her hand. "You certainly have not! You and Cliff are among my favorite people, and I'm delighted. I want ot be in on every moment of your plans. I'll be your maid of honor, won't I?"

Impulsively, Ardell leaned forward and brushed Gilyan's smooth cheek with her lips. "I wouldn't have a wedding without you! Now good night, darling. Sleep tight, and I promise not to break in again."

With the light out, Gilyan hid her wet face in the pillow to muffle her sobs.

Chapter Six

Over breakfast, that Sunday morning, Gilyan told Ardell about Vida's apology. "To say I was astonished," Gilyan said, "would be an understatement. Yet," the heavily lashed hazel eyes looked pensive, "I was more touched to receive such a reversal from Vida than I would have been from someone else."

Ardell's lips tightened. "I'm surprised, too, but *not* touched. Vida isn't my idea of a nice person!"

"She said that," Gilyan said. "Told me she wasn't a very nice person, and somehow, that's what touched me."

"Why?" Ardell's tone was uncompromising. "I don't consider it reasonable that someone cold and cutting should be thoughtless cold and cutting simply because she acknowledges those unpleasant traits."

Gilyan sighed and ran a slim hand through the coppery hair. "I just resolved," she said slowly, the fringed lids lowered over the hazel eyes, "not to be too hasty in my judgment of people, after this." The hazel eyes came up and Ardell winced at the pain in them. "I don't think I'm any judge of character."

Ardell bit back a rush of sympathy. Instead, she kept her tone brisk. "In this case, Gilyan, your original judgment was quite right. I don't think there's a female in the office who doesn't share my opinion of Vida. Furthermore, I think she might be most dangerous when she's acting contrite. Vida always has a motive for every move she makes. How Matt Groody puts up with her, I don't know."

"Alice told me she's the most efficient secretary Matt's ever had."

"Well, I'm glad she's good at something!" Ardell snapped. "As for the great love of her life not returning her love and causing her to be bitter, that's so much romantic hogwash. Hannah told me that Vida's been out for Vida since the day she first came to the paper—almost four years ago—and Tom didn't come to work for the *Globe* until a year and a half later."

Ardell changed the subject as they took their dishes to the pink tile sink and Gilyan ran hot water and poured in a capful of detergent. "Did Hannah tell you that Roy Crofton's pressuring her

71

to marry him? I don't know why she doesn't, frankly. He certainly can support her, and if Hannah waits much longer, they won't have that family they want. What is she—about thirty-five?"

"Maybe not quite that." Gilyan remembered what Hannah had said about wanting to talk to her and wondered if that was what Hannah was going to tell her.

The downstairs foyer buzzer rang, and Ardell and Gilyan looked at each other in surprise. "Who," Gilyan said, flicking off the apron protecting her bright orange capris and bulky sweater, "would be calling at this hour on Sunday morning?"

Gilyan pressed the downstairs door release and the hall buzzer sounded a few moments later. She opened the door to see a messenger with a long florist's box. Gilyan plucked a coin from the little pewter box on the wall table by the door, gave it to the boy and took the box.

Ardell was leaning over her shoulder. "Who are they from?" she asked.

Gilyan picked up the envelope with her name on it and pulled out the card. *May I call you tonight?* It was signed, *Phil Randall.* The box held long-stemmed yellow roses, a favorite of Gilyan's.

Surprised, she turned to Ardell. "How did he get my address?" she wondered.

Ardell, looking pleased, flung out her hands. "Don't ask me."

Gilyan tapped the card against even white teeth. "Now how . . .?" She broke off. "The telephone's listed under your name and I don't think it was mentioned last night that I lived with you . . ."

Ardell suddenly laughed. "I'll bet *I* know. He knew Cliff's name, and it's in the book. I'll bet he called Cliff and asked him. When Cliff calls, I'll find out."

Gilyan's brow cleared. "That must have been it."

As Ardell and Gilyan cleaned up the living room, Gilyan found herself telling Ardell about Rob Hunter. Ardell was intrigued to the point where she laid down her duster and told Gilyan to please go on.

"There isn't too much to go on," Gilyan said. "We've know each other for ages, and I guess the whole thing was one of those boy-and-girl affairs that everyone expects to evolve into marriage— and usually does."

"What's he like?" Ardell asked. "Good looking?"

"I'd say so. Rob's tall and lean and always beautifullly tanned because he's an excellent swimmer and tennis player. He's not the pretty-type handsome, but ruggedly handsome. Craggy features and very nice light-gray eyes." It was odd, but Gilyan could see him as clearly as if he were in the room. "He has very white teeth and a small cleft in his chin . . ."

"Do you have a picture of him?" Ardell wanted to know.

Gilyan laughed. "Dozens! But they're all at home."

"Well, go on. What happened? What broke it up?"

Gilyan sobered. "I guess I did. Maybe Rob was too easy, too patient, with me. I seem to need someone more—well, more decisive. Someone to lead me, if you like. Rob was more of a dreamer. He wanted to be a playwright, of all things, and I just don't think he was aggressive enough." She turned to look at Ardell. "Don't get the idea I'm being hypercritical. I'm not. Rob could most certainly write. Dad was enthusiastic about his style, but I couldn't see Rob bucking a cutthroat Broadway crowd. I'm very fond of Rob. As I told my mother, I really love him. But not as a husband. He is what I would have liked in a brother."

"I see." Ardell considered this. "And did it hurt him when you made it clear you wouldn't marry him?"

Gilyan's face clouded. "I'm afraid so. He never said a word in anger . . . Perhaps if he had, it would have been better. Perhaps if he'd told me exactly what he thought of me and . . ." She broke off. "But not Rob," she finished, almost accusingly.

74

"Do you ever hear from him?"

Gilyan shook the coppery head. "Not in ages. I asked the folks about him and they were evasive. I know Rob keeps in touch with them, and I rather think he must be engaged and, for some reason, the folks thought it would hurt me. I was—pretty unhappy when I was at home and they may have thought that would be another jolt . . ." Gilyan rested her rounded chin in her palm and stared unseeingly across the room.

"Would it have been?" Ardell asked timidly

Gilyan's mouth quirked and she leaned back against the couch. "Females are a queer lot, Ardell. It wouldn't exactly hurt—because I had my chance to marry Rob and didn't want to. Yet, at the same time, I still feel possessive about him. I guess it's just that, being so fond of him, I want him to have a girl nice enough for him."

"I wonder . . ." Ardell murmured, but Gilyan didn't hear.

Early that evening, Dr. Randall called Gilyan. Despite the frantic gestures Ardell sent in her direction, Gilyan turned him down when he asked if he could take her to dinner and a show the following night. They talked for a few minutes, she thanked him for the roses, then hung up.

"Now why," Ardell scolded, "did you do that?"

"I told you," Gilyan said quietly, "it was too soon. I haven't the energy to go out with someone and make small talk. I—well, I guess I—" To Ardell's horror, Gilyan broke into tears.

Ardell bent over her. "Oh, Gilyan! I'm such an *idiot!* Of course you don't want to go out. Poor darling. Please forgive me."

When Dr. Randall called again, later in the week, Gilyan was grateful that Ardell didn't criticize her when she turned him down. Phil Randall was polite over the telephone, but Gilyan had the feeling that he wouldn't call again. He was a very personable young man, but Gilyan knew it would be some time before she felt like meeting the challenge of a date. Going to work, immersing herself in that work and getting through the interminable nights, was enough right now. She had lost weight and was determinedly eating more and going for a brisk walk each evening. For the time being, the challenge of the day and the double challenge of the night were quite enough with which to cope. If she was living like a vegetable, then so be it.

Once she had dropped Jay's car keys into a manila envelope and sent them to the *Herald* office, Gilyan felt as though she were severing the last link between them and wished her feelings toward him could have been so easily terminated. It seemed strange, maddening, that she could still care for someone who was so shallow. But she still did care. Only once had she heard of Jay in all this time, and that indirectly. A small squib in The

Lamplighter's column, tongue-in-cheek, mentioned the heiress who surprised no one by finishing one marriage and entering another within two weeks. Perhaps the young Benedict would prove the exception, but The Lamplighter dryly stated he wasn't a betting man and didn't think exceptions ever proved anything.

However, Gilyan was gaining a bit each day. Slowly, almost imperceptibly, lapses grew between her thoughts of Jay. When they recurred, they were still painful but, like a finished piece of surgery, the scar tissue was forming and the patient knew one day nothing would remain but a fine red line, and even that would turn white with time. Gilyan waited for that time.

Chapter Seven

Two weeks later, Ardell came into the apartment after being out to a party with Cliff. She seemed excited but trying to curb it. "Gilyan?" she called, cracking the bedroom door.

Gilyan laid aside the book in her hands and leaned back against the pillows. "I'm not asleep," she said, smiling. "Come on in."

Ardell popped through the door. Her blonde hair was mussed and the round blue eyes shown with suppressed excitement. "Gilyan, guess what?"

Gilyan had to smile at her friend's eager manner. "What?"

"Dr. Randall was at the party tonight. He was with a very good-looking girl." Ardell settled herself at the foot of Gilyan's bed. "Well, as soon as he saw Cliff and me, he came right over to ask how we were. I wasn't fooled for a minute. He was hoping to hear about *you*." Ardell was violently nodding the blonde head. "Anyway, he asked me to dance later, and then he *did* ask about you. He told me how he had called you a couple of times and decided he had better not call again . . ." Ardell's enthusiasm was suddenly less noticeable. She buried herself with getting a cigarette from her purse.

Gilyan, knowing her roommate so well, folded her arms. "What did you tell him, Ardell?" But she wasn't really angry. Perhaps she would date the good doctor if he called again.

Ardell's blue eyes peered up half-defiantly, half-tearfully. "All right," she said in a rush of words. "I told him to try one more time!"

Gilyan laughed. "Honestly! You'd think I scolded you every other day and twice on Sunday!"

"You mean you're not mad?"

Gilyan sobered, shaking her head. "No," she said, "I'm not mad. I'm not exactly delirious with joy, but I'm not mad. Dr. Randall has been very patient. If he calls again, I'll probably go out with him."

"Good!" Ardell was suddenly smug. "He's calling tomorrow night."

Wednesday night, Phil Randall took Gilyan to dinner and a show and, until the time they drove back to her apartment building, Gilyan enjoyed the evening. However, as they sat in his big convertible at the curb, he suddenly put her on her guard.

"Gilyan," he said, staring straight ahead over the steering wheel and down the mist-wet street, "I don't want to spoil anything but, on the other hand, I think you should know exactly where I stand. I rather think I fell in love with you the first time I saw you."

Gilyan turned her head and met the full impact of the dark brown eyes. Her own were startled. "I know," he nodded, "you're in love with someone else. Aren't you?"

Gilyan's tongue flicked her lips. "How—how did you know?"

"There was some talk at the party the other night. Remember Bill Wilcox, the fellow who introduced us?" Numbly, Gilyan nodded her head. "He works at the *Herald*." Gilyan felt a flash of dismay. "He told me that you and Jay Hanover were practically engaged—" Phil's glance on her was concerned, gentle.

"I—see—" was all Gilyan could manage.

"Perhaps," Phil went on, "I shouldn't have said anything. However," the well-tailored shoulders shrugged, "I thought you should know." Once again, he was staring out into the street. "Jay Hanover must have been a fool!" he said softly.

"Thank you," she murmured. "I—I think you're very kind. You've paid me a compliment at a time when it means a lot to a badly damaged pride. However," her fingers twisted in her lap, "I think under the circumstances, we . . ."

His hand came firmly down on her twisting fingers. "No. Please don't say that we shouldn't see each other. I'll give my word not to mention my feelings again if you'll just continue seeing me. As I said, I thought it only honest to tell you how I feel. As far as I'm concerned, it won't be mentioned again." He smiled, and in the fused light from the mistshrouded street lamp, Gilyan noticed how warm his smile was. "Just consider me a convenient escort. Please?"

Gilyan was shaking her head at him, but she didn't remove the hand he still held so warmly. "I don't see how it would be possible for you to think that you—well, that you care for me without knowing me. I . . ."

"We weren't going to discuss this, remember? But for your edification, it was perfectly simple. I looked across the room and saw a beautiful, tall, slim girl in white, with radiant copper hair and hazel eyes with eyelashes that could be seen across the room. And that was it," he finished simply.

Gilyan looked down at their clasped hands and he withdrew his own. "I'm thirty-three," he said, "and it would be sophomoric to say I haven't been in love before. But not like this." Then, to her infinite relief, his tone lightened. "Frankly, this is the first time I've been so thoroughly snubbed!"

Gilyan raised her eyes and looked at him. His eyes were twinkling in the dim light, but she rather thought she saw a trace of pique in their dark depths. She could well believe that he wasn't used to being snubbed. Dr. Phillip Randall was more than personable and eligible. She wondered how he had managed to avoid marital snare that must have been spread before him by many unattached females. Or had he? "You've never been married?" she asked.

The dark-brown head shook. "Medical school took a lot of time, and frankly, you're the first . . ." Abruptly, he cut it short. "If I promise never to bring the subject up again—unless you should indicate it was all right—may I continue to see you?"

Slowly, Gilyan nodded. "If you like. Perhaps it isn't fair of me, feeling the way I do—did . . ." She looked down. "If you want to see me on a friendship basis, very well." She made a gesture as he started to speak. "As for your believing yourself in love with me, you've known me too briefly for that."

For a while the doctor's face wore a set look, then he smiled. "We play it your way. Friends!" He reached out and clasped Gilyan's hand, then got out of the car and came around to her side.

As they reached her door and Gilyan started inside, Phil touched her shoulder. "I," he said, looking down at her, "understand completely why you

hesitated about see me after I told you how I felt."
His look was gentle. "You're fresh from a deep
hurt and hypersensitive about causing a like hurt
to anyone else. Well, Gilyan my dear, it would
have hurt much more if you had refused to see
me." Then he smiled, nodded, and left her.

Gilyan was smiling as she let herself into the
apartment. There was a gentleness about Phil
Randall that she found very attractive. Of course
he wasn't in love with her. Perhaps he admired her
looks, or the way she dressed, but love? Not for a
moment did she think that possible. For all he
knew, she might have the disposition of a shrew.
Perhaps they could be good friends. She hoped so.

Ardell popped out of her bedroom door. Giant
rollers were on the blonde hair, a layer of cream
on her fresh-looking pink and white skin. She was
pulling a brilliantly flowered duster over equally
brilliant pajamas of bright turquoise. "He's
gone?" she hissed.

Gilyan laughed. "You look like you just came
in on a fast schedule from Mars!"

Ardell brushed this aside. "Well, did you have
fun? Is Dr. Randall as nice as he seems?" She
plumped herself down on an arm of the couch.

"Honestly, Ardell! Of course he's nice. But
don't let those romantic hopes of yours run away
with you!"

Ardell refused to be daunted. "He has the *most
beautiful* manners. And the way he dresses. A

kind of quiet elegance, without being foppish. How did he ever go this long without being snatched up by some strong-willed female?" Fortunately, Ardell didn't pause long enough for Gilyan to have to supply any answers. "And the way he notices whatever you're wearing! Before you came in, he even noticed my old black lounging pajamas; made dumpy little old me feel positively svelte, and without sounding like he was spreading it on. What a talent! If Cliff had walked in just then, I'd have walked up to him without a word and belted him. I could wear a potato sack and he wouldn't notice the difference." Ardell sighed lustily. "Then when you walked in in that lime silk—ah! I don't think he missed a detail. Dr. Randall, my friend, is one of a vanishing breed." Ardell hastily added, "In your case, nothing he could say would be an exaggeration. That lime color, with your hair, has to be seen to be believed."

Gilyan flushed. "Ardell, please don't get your hopes up. Dr. Randall and I are going to be friends. Just—friends."

Ardell's round face, under the rolle-up hair, looked as severe as it possibly could. "Gilyan, I saw the way Dr. Randall looked at you—and it *wasn't* platonic."

Gilyan sobered. "I hope I didn't make a mistake in saying I'd see him again," she murmured, half to herself.

Ardell pounced. "Ha! So he does like you more than just as a friend."

Gilyan, worried as to whether or not she had made the right decision, told Ardell what had happened downstairs in the car. Ardell's eyes sparkled. "Of course you did the right thing," she said heartily, and Gilyan knew she would get no constructive advice from her roommate. Ardell was hoping that, given time, Phil Randall could restore her bruised heart.

Sighing, Gilyan got ready for bed.

On Thursday, Gilyan was surprised and touched to have Julia Caldwell ask if she could take her to lunch. Over lunch, Julia mentioned the basket of fruit she had received from Ardell and Gilyan.

"I was so pleased when the basket came," she said in her soft voice. The lovely slanted eyes glowed. "I felt better just receiving it."

Gilyan felt a small lump in her throat. After all this time, Julia was still talking about the basket of fruit, a girl like Julia, who should, in the ordinary course of events, be barraged with gifts from beaus. Impulsively, she asked, "Do you get out much, Julia?" She had phrased it badly, and amended, "Sometimes Ardell's boy friend asks if we can find a date for one of his friends so I just wondered if you ever dated that way?" This left Julia a graceful out. If she didn't approve of blind dates, she should be able to tell Gilyan. If, on the other hand, the poor girl didn't get an opportunity to date, this would be that opportunity. If Cliff didn't know someone eligible, perhaps Phil Randall would.

Julia sipped her coffee, then gave Gilyan a start. "Oh," she smiled, setting down her cup, "didn't you know I went steadily with a boy?" As Gilyan, trying to hide her surprise, shook her head, Julia leaned confidentially forward. "Oh, yes. Very much so. We've been going together for almost a year. But we're keeping it quiet. My aunt, you know."

Gilyan didn't know why, but she was quite suddenly, and completely, convinced that Julia was lying. The long amber eyes looking into hers were perfectly clear and steady, the soft smile turning up the rosy mouth was just the smile it should be, and yet Gilyan was so convinced that Julia was lying she couldn't bring herself to ask any of the normal questions. Then her blankness dissolved in a deeper wave of pity. Julia was compensating. She couldn't date as other girls did but, in order to conceal this fact, she made up a beau. Pride made people do strange things, and Gilyan had no desire to force poor Julia into compounding her face-saving lie by asking her to describe her mythical swain. She looked down at her watch with an exclamation.

"Julia! Just as the conversation gets interesting,

we have to run." Did she see relief in the a... eyes across from her? Gilyan thought so. Keeping her tone light, she said, "And by the way, Julia, I'll keep your secret. In fact, we won't mention it again until you can let us all in on it. Okay?"

Julia smiled. "Thank you, Gilyan."

Gilyan took out her wallet. "The lunch was wonderful and thank you so much, but I insist on leaving the tip." She wished she could have taken the tab for the lunch, too, but that might have hurt Julia's feelings.

That night, there was excitement at the apartment. Cliff had received his draft notice for the following month, and he and Ardell decided to marry a week from next Saturday. They would drive to Reno; then, after the ceremony, he and Ardell, who had a two-week vacation due her, would go on a honeymoon.

"You'll go with us?" Ardell turned to Gilyan. Her already rosy face flushed a deeper pink. "I mean to Reno—for our wedding?"

Gilyan nodded, smiling. 'Of course I'll go. I can drive up with you two, then come back on a plane that night, or early the next morning. I wouldn't think of missing it."

Shortly afterward, treading on air, Cliff and Ardell left to go over to see Cliff's father.

As soon as they had left, Gilyan put in a call to her mother, to tell her the news. Mrs. Barr was delighted. "I just wish we could be here a week from Saturday," Gilyan's parents were returning to England on Monday, "and we'd fly down for the wedding. However, we'll bring them something from England. Does Ardell have her china?"

"No. Frankly, she doesn't have too much of anything. I think they'd love English china."

"How are you feeling?" Her mother's tone hid concern. "Is—is everything all right with you, dear?"

"Yes. I dated a Dr. Phil Randall and found myself enjoying the evening." Gilyan changed the subject. "How long will you and Daddy be gone?"

"Just long enought for him to clear up some tag ends. We hope to be back under two weeks. They're starting the patio work about then at the house, and I'd like to be here. You'll be up then, won't you?"

"Yes. I plan on taking a week of my vacation after you get back. It'll work out nicely. Ardell will be away for two weeks—after next week-end —and I should be able to get my week in just before, or just after, she returns."

They talked a few more minutes, then said goodbye, and Gilyan slept much better that night, better than she had in a long while.

Chapter Eight

Saturday night, when Phil called to pick up Gilyan, he brought a corsage of small green orchids and a box of liqueur chocolates. The orchids went well on Gilyan's chiffon dress of muted pink with mauve undertones. The coppery hair lay in softly bouffed wings, a narrow velvet band above the shining waves that exactly matched the deeper rose of her silk pumps. As Phil stepped back after pinning the corsage to one softly drapped strap crossing her shoulder, Gilyan felt her face flush at the admiration in his eyes. However, his tone was almost brisk.

"You look radiant, Miss Barr. It will be a pleasure to be seen with you on my arm."

Gilyan nodded her head. "Thank you, Doctor." She lifted the foiled box. "Where ever in San Francisco did you get the liqueur chocolates?

Mother and Dad always bring me some when they return from London. I'm very fond of them."

"In that case, I'll keep my source of supply a secret and you'll have to depend on my getting them for you. Shall we go?" Suddenly he looked anxious. "Friends of mine, Sandra and Bill Haviland, are going with us tonight. Do you mind?"

Gilyan was careful to hide her pleasure. She had been rather dreading spending the evening alone with Phil, still not completely convinced that he would keep the more personal element out of their friendship. Now she could relax, look forward to the evening with enjoyment.

Sandra and Bill Haviland were a delightful couple. Sandra, slim, tanned, and blonde; not beautiful, but so poised and elegantly groomed, she gave the illusion of beauty. It was obvious that her handsome, dark-haired husband adored her. And both of them seemed to like Gilyan on sight.

They had dinner on the roof of one of the big hotels, then danced until after one in the morning. Gilyan felt, by evening's end, that she had known Bill and Sandra for a long time and promised Sandra, on parting, that they would lunch together soon.

As Phil left Gilyan at her door, he brought up the subject of Ardell's wedding. "You say you're going up with them next week-end, then coming back Sunday, alone, on the plane?"

Gilyan nodded. "I certainly couldn't miss Ardell's wedding."

The dark eyes looked thoughtful, then alert. "Look. My week-end's free. Why couldn't we drive up there together?" His enthusiasm mounted. "I could drive you up Saturday and bring you back Sunday. That is," he added, "if Ardell and Cliff wouldn't mind my being there?"

Gilyan smiled. "I'm sure they wouldn't. In fact, I think they would like it. It will be such a small wedding. You see, Cliff's father can't go. He has a heart condition and has to stay out of high altitudes."

"I'll have my secretary call Monday and make reservations for us at the Riverside for Saturday night. Okay?"

"Yes, if I pay for my room," Gilyan said firmly.

He looked for a moment as though an objecton was on the tip of his tongue, then he capitulated. "Very well, Miss-Mind-of-Your-Own. I'll call you Monday night and let you know if we have our reservations."

When Gilyan told her, Ardell was delighted. "Oh, Gilyan, I couldn't be more pleased. He's such a nice person and you won't have to come back by yourself on Sunday. And it will be such a small wedding. We wanted to change our plans when we found that Cliff's dad couldn't go, but he insisted that we not change them."

Monday morning, Gilyan stopped by Hannah's desk. "Didn't you say you wanted to tell me something? We've been so busy, I almost forgot about it."

Hannah leaned back and lit a cigarette. "I almost forgot myself. Yes, when this rat race calms down a bit, I do want to talk with you. But actually, there's no hurry and I'd like to get a few more details settled before going into it. Maybe—just maybe—we can manage one of these fine days to get away at the same time for lunch. Okay?"

Gilyan nodded. "Do you realize we haven't had lunch together for a couple of months?"

Hannah's dark eyes twinkled up at her. "And don't you realize *why?*"

Blankly, Gilyan shook her head. "No. Why?"

Hannah gave a shout of laughter and ran destructive hands through the gray-brown hair, causing it to stand on end. "Oh, my good hat! Maybe I shouldn't have said anything. Gilyan, haven't you noticed how many of *my* assignments I've been giving you to cover?" As Gilyan continued to look blank, Hannah lowered her voice, but she still sounded amused. "Don't you realize that in the past two months I've been handing you more and more of the *big* weddings, the important social events, to cover?"

"Well—I know I've been busy," Gilyan said.

"I should hope so!" Hannah snorted, lighting a fresh cigarette as Gilyan automatically reached out to snub the one in the ash tray. "That," she lowered her voice still more, "has something to do with what I want to talk to you about. But I think we can delay the talk until Ardell gets back from her honeymoon." She laid down the new cigarette and ran both hands through her hair, with disastrous results. "What I'm going to do without her," she moaned, "I don't know. Julia's going to help me."

The week passed quickly for Gilyan. She wondered, as she sped from lunch speaker to dinner speaker to business women's luncheon to author's teas, that she hadn't noticed before how much outside coverage she had been doing recently. Could it mean that Hannah might be planning to marry, to step down? Gilyan couldn't visualize Hannah quietly remaining in a house or an apartment, doing housework, after the hectic years she had put in on the paper. Yet Hannah could very well be tired of the grind. The thought of being able to plan and prepare meals to be eaten in the peace of one's own home might be tremendously appealing after years of covering the social merry-go-round.

The trip to Reno started out on a high note. Dr. Randall picked Gilyan up around one in the afternoon. Ardell and Cliff had left earlier in order to complete their final arrangements for the eight o'clock wedding.

It was hot coming through the Sacramento Valley, but beyond Auburn, climbing out of the foothills and into the mountains, the air was clear and crisp and cool. The scenery over the High Sierras was beautiful. As they topped the summit to drop down to Donner, Gilyan pulled a white angora sweater on over her moss-green sheath. They had stopped just outside Truckee for coffee and it was six-thirty by the time they reached the Riverside.

Gilyan stopped by Ardell's room, then went to her own room to shower and change. She put on a beige silk, two-piece suit with a short jacket. There were gloves and smart cloche, in tissue-silk leaves, of soft green. She picked up her beige bag and slipped her feet into beige silk pumps and carried her mink stole. The air in Reno already had a bite to it.

Phil's eyes lighted as she came into the big foyer. "It isn't fair," he said quietly, his eyes sweeping over her. "It just isn't fair to the bride."

Gilyan's face felt hot, and he quickly added, "I insisted that Cliff let me get yours and Ardell's flowers. Come in and help."

They went into the flower shop and Gilyan selected for herself more of the small green orchids. Ardell's orchids were white, intermingled with lilies of the valley and white satin streamer, Gilyan put her flowers on and they took Ardell's with them in their transparent box.

At the Chapel, Gilyan had a few bad moments during the ceremony when the thick feeling in her throat threatened to engulf her; however, when she looked at Ardell and Cliff, the way they were looking at each other, the radiant happiness that was almost tangible, she immediately brought herself out of it. For the first time, she noticed that Phil had taken her hand. She turned her head to look at him and saw by the look he sent back that he understood what she was feeling. His gesture was one of reassurance. Gilyan smiled her thanks.

Phil had arranged for a quiet champagne supper, and immediately afterward, Ardell and Cliff were on their way. Ardell clutched Gilyan for a moment before she climbed into Cliff's car. "Gilyan," she whispered, "everything will work out for you, too! One of these days you'll be as happy as I am."

Swallowing, Gilyan kissed her and blew another kiss toward the beaming Cliff, and they were gone.

"Now," Phil's tone was light, "shall we shake Reno up and do a bit of gambling?"

"Of course." Gilyan fell in with his mood. "I think we should let Reno know we've been here."

It was in one of the big casinos that Gilyan's happy mood was shattered into a thousand pieces. She was watching Phil at the dice table. Not knowing the game, Gilyan had said that she preferred to watch. Suddenly, over the cacophony of sound —the click of roulette wheels, the jangle of coins, the rattle of dice and clang of slot machines—she heard a shout of jubilation and, with others at the table, turned to look toward a table farther back. The girl who had given the whoop of triumph was Nancy Covington Hanover.

She was surrounded by a group of men and women, and her face was full of glee as she looked down on a tossed pair of dice. Her furs were half off bare shoulders, showing a décolleté dress of dully shimmering silver, much the same color as the high-piled hair. To Gilyan's right, a woman said distinctly and somewhat resentfully, "That's the Covington heiress. Them that has—gets! But maybe the old saying, "Lucky in cards, unlucky in love,' is right. She's up here to shed her fourth husband."

The woman's companion shrilled, "Her *fourth?* I'm behind times. I saw her up here not too long ago, shedding a third. Who's the fourth?"

"Oh, some newspaperman," the first woman answered carelessly. "His name's Hancock—or something like that."

Blindly, Gilyan turned. All she wanted was to get out of the place. She started for one of the exits.

Out in the fresh air, she was surprised to look up and see that Phil was with her. Without a word, he had her arm and was signaling a taxi, giving the driver the name of their hotel.

In the cab, he held her hand tightly. "Would you like to go back to San Francisco tonight?" he asked.

Gilyan took a deep breath and shook her head. "No. No . . . You've had a long drive today and I know you're tired. I—I just want to go up to my room."

At the hotel, he made Gilyan sit down in the foyer. "I'll be right back," he said. When he returned, he accompanied her up to her door, where he took a small envelope from his pocket.

"I've put two sleeping tablets in here, Gilyan. One should do. However, if it doesn't, you may take the second." He looked down and with the sympathy in his eyes made her own eyes fill. "Now go to bed," he said. "Take a tepid bath, the first pill, and go directly to bed."

Gilyan started through the door, but turned back. She was surprised to find that her voice was hoarse. "Phil . . . Phil, you're very kind. I really thank you."

The drive back to San Francisco was far different from the drive up. Phil turned on the car radio and said very little during the drive down. Gilyan leaned back, trying to doze. What was she feeling? Was there, in the mixture of emotions, a bitter feeling of triumph that Jay had been taken for a lightning ride of delusion by Nancy Minx

Covington? That he had gotten just what he asked for? But if there was any triumph in Gilyan's thoughts, it held small consolation. If Jay's love hadn't been the shallow emotion it was, he and Gilyan right now would be planning their marriage. The thought that tore at Gilyan was a recurring question: If Jay had never met Nancy, would *their* marriage have worked out? Nancy could have been an infatuation that hit him like a bolt of lightning. Even while Gilyan thought this, she knew it wasn't right. If you genuinely love one person, you don't become involved with another. Unless—hadn't Ardell called him an opportunist? Hadn't she intimated that he liked to use people in order to further himself? That he was too fond of money? This all jibed. But somehow, it made the whole thing seem much worse.

Gilyan was suddenly asleep. And later, it would occur to her that during that sleep, coming down from Reno, she slept some of the pain and disillusionment away. The pain would return at intervals, but never so acutely again.

Chapter Nine

Gilyan missed Ardell.

During the first week, Phil took her out twice and both times brought her a small gift. More of the liqueur chocolates the first time, and when she protested, half-laughingly, that he would ruin her complexion, he brought her a slim golden compact on their next date, and Gilyan didn't have the heart to demur.

They had three dates the following week, and a tentative one for Saturday, but Phil called and told her he had an emergency at the hospital and would have to cancel it. He sounded so apologetic that Gilyan quickly assured him that it was perfectly all right and she would see him the following Monday. He asked about Ardell, and Gilyan told him she wouldn't be back until Monday. Matt had given the bride an extra day.

Sunday afternoon, Gilyan was surprised to have a phone call from Julia. Julia sounded rather hesitant. "Gilyan, I just found myself with a free afternoon. A relative dropped in, from out of town, to visit with Aunt Grita. Are you doing anything?"

Gilyan asked Julia if she could come over and have dinner with her. Sounding pleased, Julia said she would like that, but added that she couldn't stay late.

Gilyan prepared a rolled steak, dollar-sized potato pancakes, and shrimp salad. Over their ices and coffee, Julia was still exclaiming over the apartment. And Gilyan found herself wondering what Julia's living quarters must be like. Julia, as though reading her thoughts, supplied the answer.

"Aunt Grita would feel so much better in a cheery place like this," she said, looking around at the soft yellow walls. "We have one of those hideous old apartments that seem to pick up the foggy, gray days and bring them inside. However," Julia sighed, "Perhaps one day . . ."

Gilyan felt sorry for her. "Does Matt know you're taking care of an invalid aunt? Isn't it possible he might do better on your salary?"

Julia's amber eyes widened. "Mr. Groody? I wouldn't *think* of asking him. What if he should say—'If you don't like this job, you're free to get another, better paying one'?"

"What if he did?" Gilyan persisted. "Perhaps you *could* get another job that paid you better."

Julia shook her head. "I'm working to fulfill a dream," she said. "A dream I've had ever since I was a child." The slanted eyes weren't seeing Gilyan; they seemed to be looking inward. "I want to write, to be a woman columnist, one day."

"What kind of column do you want to do?" Gilyan asked.

Julia focused her eyes. "Oh. When I'm qualified, I'd like a job like Hannah's, and the chance to work into a specialized column of my own. I don't mean to sound presumptuous, but I'd like to do profiles on people like The Lamplighter does— from a woman's viewpoint."

Jay had said much the same thing about wanting to do a column like The Lamplighter. Gilyan kept her dismay from her face. "But, Julia, I rather think The Lamplighter must have a writing background."

Julia didn't look at all daunted. "I think so, too. But I *can*—given the opportunity—learn to write! Can you keep a secret?" Gilyan nodded. "I'm taking a writing course now. I arranged with our landlady to sit with Aunt Grita twice a week, and I'm working very hard. My teacher, Mr. Himes, says that my weak point is description, but that I'm very good on dialogue and continuity. I intend to learn to write—and when I do . . ." Her soft chin jutted.

"And when you do?" Gilyan prodded.

"If I don't make the grade, it won't be for lack of trying!" The grim look left Julia's face and she laughed. "Oh, Gilyan, what you must think of me. I sound like an awful egotist."

"I don't think you do at all," Gilyan said firmly. "I envy you. You know what you want and are going after it. That's laudable."

Julia looked wistful. "I wish I could write copy as well as you do."

"If I do copy at all well, it's because I've been raised on writing. You see, my father is not only a newspaperman, but does articles as well. My mother has written at least twenty-five fooks—fiction—and I've been living with the clack of typewriters for most of my life. I couldn't help but absorb something."

"How I envy you!" Julia leaned forward. "Do you think it's possible for someone to learn to write at my age?"

Gilyan nodded. "Dad has often said that writing is like tennis or piano playing. All it takes is constant practice. That anyone, with a reasonable facility of vocabulary, can learn to write if they do it regularly."

Julia's eyes danced. "I knew it," she said. "I've been writing each night, and I swear I can tell the difference. Here . ." She scrambled in her bag and brought out some pieces of copy paper. "Would you read this?"

Gilyan recognized copy on one of the weddings she had covered some weeks ago. For a moment, she thought it her own, then realized it wasn't. She looked up. "Did you write this?"

Julia nodded. "I've been taking old copy of yours, getting the salient facts, then doing it over in my words. Can you notice any improvement?"

The degree of improvement was astonishing. "Julia, these are excellent! You're developing a style of your own. How long have you been attending the writing class?"

"A couple of months." She spread her hands. "I never said anything before because I didn't know whether I had improved enough. But the other night, Mr. Himes said he thought I was ready for advanced work."

"I would certainly agree," Gilyan said. "Why don't you wait another week—until Ardell's back —then ask Hannah if you can't try doing more assignments?"

Julia leaned forward to touch Gilyan's hand. "I want a bit more time. Please keep my secret." She smiled. "I know what Hannah thinks of my past efforts. I know that you and Hannah practically had to rewrite everything I did." She twinkled. "Elmer kept me posted. That's why I took the course. I knew I'd have to produce better writing if I wanted to get started on my goal. You see, Gilyan, up till a couple of months ago, I just kind of *dreamed* my dream. Then suddenly it struck me—Don't dream! Do it! That's why I don't want to ask for a raise. I may not be making much, mut at least I have a toehold in a newspaper office." She touched the tucks of pale lavender in her smart crepe dress. "My cousins take care of me in the clothing department, bless them, so I can manage until I get a break."

Gilyan understood many things about Julia in that moment. She realized that under the soft exterior, there was an amazing drive, an ambition that should, by the law of averages, work out for her.

Gilyan indicated the copy paper. "Why don't you let me show these to Hannah?"

Julia shook her head, the set look vanishing. "Oh, no, not yet." She took the papers from Gilyan's fingers and put them in her purse. "I really need a bit more time. But when I feel the time is right, I would appreciate it if you'd put in a word for me."

"Of course I will," Gilyan said.

"And you won't say anything to Hannah until I ask you?" Julia pleaded.

Gilyan solemnly raised her right hand. "I promise."

Julia rose. "I can't tell you how much I've enjoyed myself, but I must run along now."

As Gilyan went to the guest closet in the foyer for Julia's coat, she knew by the way Julia caressed the soft folds that it was new. When Julia came in, they had been greeting each other as Gilyan automatically took the coat and put it in the closet. Now she reached out to touch the silky cashmere in deep violet with a wide shawl collar.

"What a *beautiful* coat!" she said.

Julia hugged it about her slimness and turned. "Isn't it? It looks practically new, doesn't it?" She sobered. "Sometimes I think Jill tires of things quickly just for my benefit." She arched a slender foot in soft bone kid. "I can even wear Jill's shoes. A perfect fit."

Phil called five minutes after Julia left. "I just heard from Sandra Haviland," he said. "She and Bill would like us over for some bridge. I told her I hadn't asked you out tonight because I expected to be busy, but I find I'm not. Would you be free to go over there with me?"

Gilyan said she would be glad to go and could be ready by eight. She hadn't taken two steps away from the teleephone when it rang again, a long, strident ring. The long-distance operator said she had a call for Miss Gilyan Barr from Guaymas, Mexico.

Gilyan, puzzled as to whom could be calling her from the fishing hamlet in Mexico, identified herself and waited. Then the walls seemed to swoop in on her. It was Jay.

"Hello, Gilyan?" The connection was bad, but Gilyan, closing her eyes tightly and holding the receiver so hard that her knuckles turned white, knew his voice instantly. "Gilyan?" he repeated.

Over a tight throat, she answered: "Yes—it's Gilyan."

"I wouldn't blame you if you hung up on me, Gilyan." Jay's voice came faintly. "I wouldn't blame you in the least."

She cleared her throat. "I won't hang up. What did you want?"

"I . . ." For the first time, he sounded hesitant. "I guess I just wanted to hear your voice. Not that I deserve to."

There seemed nothing to say to that so Gilyan waited, the room gradually stopping its slow spin.

"I—I'm coming back to San Francisco in a week or so. I have a chance to do some free-lance work for one of the Chicago papers—that's what I'm doing down here—and I want to stop by and see Coulter at the *Herald*. May I—please—may I see you then, too, Gilyan?"

Gilyan shook her head, then spoke almost sharply: "No, Jay! No. It would accomplish nothing." She felt the tears welling and quickly added, "This call is accomplishing nothing. Goodbye, Jay." She hung up before the tears came.

They were painful tears, like the reopening of a wound. Once they subsided, Gilyan walked into her bedroom and looked at her ravaged face. She couldn't possibly go out with Phil tonight. Before she could think about it, she picked up the bedside telephone and dialed his number.

"Phil?" she said thickly. "This is rude, but please don't ask me to explain. I can't go to the Havilands' with you tonight." Before he could say anything, she dropped the handset into its cradle and sank down on the edge of the bed.

Gilyan didn't know how long she had sat there, in the dusk-filled room, when she heard the sound of the hallway buzzer. At first, she ignored its summons, but as it continued to rip through the apartment, she got to her feet and walked into the small foyer.

"Who is it?" she called through the door.

"Gilyan, let me in," Phil said quietly.

Gilyan opened the door, and without a word, Phil took her into his arms, gently smoothing one of the trembling shoulders. Gilyan had thought herself cried out long ago, but the warm sympathy in Phil's voice, his touch, seemed to tap a fresh wellspring of tears.

"Now," Phil said gently, as Gilyan ducked her head, "you go in and wash your face. I'll be making some hot chocolate. Then you're going to get yourself a book and into bed and relax. If you want me to sit out in the living room until you get to sleep, I'll be glad to do it. If you want me to go, I'll do that, too."

Gilyan pressed his hand. "I—I'm glad you came, but it won't be necessary for you to stay.

I'm—I'm sorry to disappoint the Havilands, and I'd feel better about it if you didn't."

"If you want me to go over, of course I will. But wouldn't you like me to fix you some hot chocolate first? I'm very good at making chocolate."

Gilyan gave a shaky laugh. "I'm sure you are. But, no. I'll have a tepid bath and take that second little pill you gave me that night in Reno." She blotted her face with a handkerchief from the pocket of her blue velvet lounging coat. "Okay, Doctor?"

"Okay," he said, and, bending, dropped a kiss on her forehead. He turned at the door. "I'll call you."

Gilyan stared at the closed door. Another plus to be notched up for Phil Randall. Along with his gentle thoughtfulness was an innate tact. Fervently, Gilyan wished she could care for him as she had for Jay. Her mother had expressed it in the old cliche: Love wasn't some tap labeled hot and cold that one could turn on or off at will.

Chapter Ten

The next morning when Gilyan entered Hannah's office to cross to her own, her face, above the slim sheath of sheer black wool, looked paler, almost luminous and just slightly darker than the pearl choker clasped about her throat, but her step was brisk, her look bright as she greeted Hannah.

Hannah stretched luxuriously. "What a way to start the day—early!" she said.

Gilyan paused by her desk. "You *are* early. Any special reason?" Hannah usually went to her first assignment directly from her apartment. Sometimes it was afternoon before she got to the office. However, Hannah was usually at her desk, answering the mail for next day's Question Box, long after the rest of them went home.

"Oh," Hannah lit a cigarette, "I wanted to see how the other half lives. Our little bride," she digressed, "will be in Tuesday—tomorrow—won't she?"

Gilyan nodded. "Yes. Cliff reports to Fort Ord. I'll be glad to have her back."

"So will I. Not," Hannah hastily qualified, "that Julia hasn't done a darn good job of filling in." Hannah's expression showed mild surprise. "And you know what? Julia's improving in the writing department!" Gilyan tried to look equally surprised. "I had to leave to meet the incoming royalty the other night and still had two letters to answer from the Question Box. Julia offered to do them, so what could I say? Naturally, I figured I'd do them over the next morning and run 'em a day late. But I didn't have to. She said she just made herself think like me, and answered their questions."

Gilyan was delighted. If Hannah could find out on her own that Julia was improving, so much the better.

Gilyan was further pleased a bit later in the morning when Sandra Haviland called and asked if they might have lunch together. She was downtown and could meet Gilyan wherever convenient. Attending a tea and fashion show later in the day, Gilyan was glad she had worn the loosely belled white hopsacking coat, with its bold black and white print lining, over the black sheath. A large black patent bag and slim-heeled patent pumps completed the outfit.

110

Sandra Haviland was in a short-jacketed blue wool suit under soft furs that highlighted her even tan and light-blue eyes. The blonde hair gleamed under a winged blue hat. "Gilyan!" She held out both hands in their immaculate white gloves. "It's so nice to see you again." She drew back. "Great shades of night! You're even prettier than I remembered!" Her tone, amusingly enough, verged on the accusing.

Gilyan laughed. "We must be a mutual-admiration committee. You just beat me to it."

Sandra gave the throaty chuckle that so intrigued Gilyan. "Look, Sweetie, I know my limitations. However," she shrugged, "I can do a lot with the aid of the better cosmetic firms and a good boutique."

Over lunch, Sandra told Gilyan how disappointed she and Bill were the night before when she didn't come with Phil; she was sorry she had had such a bad headache. Gilyan sent a silent thanks to Phil for making the excuse. Then Sandra said lightly, "that's the way to treat the young bucko."

Gilyan didn't follow the words, or the too-light tone. "What do you mean?"

Sandra fanned orange-tipped fingers. "Oh, I just mean these attractive young males need to be stood up once in a while. Good deflationary measures."

For a moment, Gilyan was taken aback. Didn't Sandra like Phil?

Some of her feeling must have shown in her face, for Sandra laughed and said, "Oh, don't get me wrong. I'm very fond of Dr. Randall. But sometimes I think, with the single female population what it is, our unattached males need to be gently trod on once in a while." She suddenly sobered and dropped her voice. "It's none of my business, of course, but that won't stop me from asking, because I think you and I share one of those solid and instant rapports." Gilyan conceded this with a nod and waited. "Are you pretty fond of Phil?" Sandra's expression told her exactly nothing.

Slowly, carefully, Gilyan answered: "Fond of him? Yes. Phil's a very thoughtful and kind person. But it *is* only fondness on my part."

For a long moment, the only sound was the subdued clatter of china, the clink of silver and murmur of conversation around them. Sandra was looking down at the ash tray where she was depositing a cigarette stub. "I see," she finally said. Was she disappointed? Gilyan couldn't tell. Then the blue eyes came up and their regard became intent on Gilyan's face. "Is there someone else, Gilyan?" Swiftly, she added, "You certainly don't need to answer that if you think I'm prying."

"I don't think you're prying. Yes, there is someone else. It isn't working out, but there is someone else."

For a moment, Gilyan thought Sandra was going to say something further, something that she very much wanted to say, but the moment passed and Sandra changed the subject to her own hobby of painting. The hour passed quickly and pleasantly, and when they parted, Sandra made Gilyan promise to come out to the house soon, with or without Phil.

In the taxi, going back to the *Globe*, Gilyan went over the byplay between herself and Sandra. Were Sandra and Bill worried about the welfare of Dr. Phil Randall? Did they sense how he felt about Gilyan, and were they afraid she might hurt him? Had Sandra been about to tell her that, then reconsidered? The thought made Gilyan uncomfortable and she felt relieved that Sandra hadn't continued with the subject.

A radiant Ardell was there when Gilyan got home Monday night. They talked until well after midnight. Cliff had left that afternoon for Fort Ord—some of the sparkle faded—she wouldn't see him for six weeks, but they rather thought, Ardell brightened, that if he were sent to a passable station, she would join Cliff in about six months. After all, two years was a long time and if she worked another six months and saved the allotment she would receive from the Government, they should be able to manage nicely. Especially if Cliff was stationed near a town large enough to have a daily newspaper. Matt would surely give Ardell a good recommendation.

"Of course he will," Gilyan agreed. "And as much as I hate thinking of the day you go, I know you're doing the right thing. Two years can be an awfully long time." She had another thought. "When Cliff does start to get week-end passes, you just let me know a couple of days ahead and I'll make a hotel reservation . . ."

"You'll do no such thing!" Ardell exclaimed. "*We* can go to a hotel."

Gilyan shook her head. "You and Cliff will stay right here. Then you won't have to eat out. You can play house and cook his meals."

Ardell's blue eyes twinkled at her roommate. "May I say—for the thousandth time—what a dear I think you are?"

Gilyan decided to get the subject they had skirted for hours out into the open. "Did you read about Jay and Nancy Covington?" she asked.

Instantly, Ardell sobered. "Yes. She must have been in Reno around the time we were there."

"She was. Nancy Covington Hanover was playing at a dice table just behind us. I heard two women talking about her—and that's when I learned she was getting a divorce from Jay. Incidentally," Gilyan busied herself with lighting a cigarette, "Jay called here the other night. From Guaymas."

"Oh, no!" Ardell cried. "Oh, Gilyan. How could he? You *didn't* say you'd see him?"

Gilyan shook her head. "I did not."

"Thank heaven! What was he doing in Guaymas? Is—is he coming back to San Francisco?"

"He may be coming here briefly, but apparently he's working on a Chicago paper. I heard, through the grapevine, that Coulter was pretty angry about the way Jay quit. I understand he just sent Coulter a wire, saying he was through."

"I should think he would be angry!" Ardell snapped. "After all, he was Coulter's representative at the series, and that left him high and dry. Editors aren't noted for liking such a performance."

"Maybe," Gilyan kept her tone light, "he's going to try to make his peace with Coulter."

"Did he ask to see you?" Ardell asked in a tight voice.

"Yes. But I refused."

Ardell changed the subject. "How are you and Phil getting along?"

"Fine. He's a thoroughly nice person."

"Do you . . ." Ardell's face turned pink. "Do you ever feel that you might be growing fond of him?"

Gilyan sighed. "I am fond of Phil, but I know what you're trying to ask. Honestly, Ardell, I just don't know. I feel—numb. Right now, my emotions are dulled—not unpleasantly. Frankly, I would just as soon they stayed that way for a while." Gilyan's worry lay in the fear that the numbness might vanish, the emotion return with a rush at sight of Jay—and deep within her lay a conviction that she would see Jay Hanover soon. The feeling was half-dread and, hating herself for the admission, half-anticipation.

Chapter Eleven

Two days later, Hannah came into Gilyan's office and they had their talk.

Hannah folded her slim length into the chair across from Gilyan's desk. "There's more privacy in here," she said. "Now I can tell what's been on my mind." Hannah lit a cigarette and started. Roy Crofton, her long-patient fiancé, had finally put his foot down. He wanted Hannah to marry him around the first of year, which gave her time to get her business affairs in order.

"This is what I should like." Hannah leaned forward. "I want *you* to step into my place. Perhaps I don't have the final word—Matt does. But he likes you, and with the quality of your work and a plan I have—it should be a shoo-in."

Gilyan stirred restively, flattered, yet wanting

117

to be fair. "Have you considered Julia? She's been here longer than I have."

Hannah scowled at the smoke curling up from her cigarette. "In all fairness, yes. I considered her, but I'm afraid that I did it from purely sympathetic reasons. I think improvement on her part would have to be somewhat phenomenal for her to make the grade." Hannah put out her cigarette and lighted another. "As I said, it won't be entirely up to me. I've been giving you more and more responsibility, but I would like something concrete to take into Matt. Could you dream up some kind of a promotional campaign? Matt's a sucker for anything civic minded, and when you get it licked into shape, you can show it to me and we'll go over it. This should give you a good month or two to work on it. I don't intend to tell Matt—or anyone else—that I'm leaving until a few weeks before I actually leave."

Although grateful, Gilyan still felt a small prickle of conscience where Julia was concerned. An opportunity like this would mean everything in the world to the girl, and heaven knew Julia's world held little enough of hope. Yet Gilyan could understand Hannah's decision. Gilyan had promised Julia that she wouldn't reveal her secret about the writing course, but she could, perhaps, help in another way.

"Hannah, you said Julia was doing a better job of writing. If I should move up when you go, Julia might be able to work into my job. Let's give her another try. The Scanlon wedding is coming up Saturday. Why not assign her to that?"

Hannah hesitated, then nodded the gray-brown head. "Okay. I'll tell her. Now when you start in on this promotional deal, tell me if and when you need additional time. It won't be necessary to give me progress reports. I know your work and I know what it's like to be pressured; I'd much rather see a finished product. And keep the whole thing under your hat. I don't want this to . . ." Hannah's head came up, her hand froze over the ash tray. She spun about, to look at the slightly ajar door leading into Gilyan's office.

"What is it?" Gilyan asked.

Hannah rose from her chair in one lithe movement and crossed to the door. She flung it wide, looked out, then slowly returned. "I thought I heard someone," she said tersely. "And I would swear I closed your door tightly when I came in."

"Gilyan?" he said. "I'm sorry to disturb you at you sure?"

Hannah's mouth narrowed. "Pretty sure. I don't want word of any of this to get to Matt until I tell him myself . . ." Hannah's face was still perturbed as she abruptly went back to her office.

Gilyan's phone rang, and she was surprised to hear Phil's voice.

"Gilyan?" he said. "I'm sorry to disturb you at

119

work, but I have to fly down to Miami for a week. I just found out. Would you like to drive me out to the airport tonight? My plane leaves at eight so we could have dinner out there before I leave."

'I'll miss you," Gilyan said without thinking, and then realized just how true this would be. Before he could speak, she added, "Is this a pleasure trip?"

"Not really. There's a convention down there and I'm presenting a paper for Dr. Jorgensen. At the last minute, he couldn't make it."

Gilyan said she would leave the office early and that he could pick her up at the apartment around six. "Why don't you let me drive you out in my car? Then you can leave yours in the garage."

"I thought you might like to use my car while I'm gone," he said. Again, comparison arose as Gilyan recalled the way Jay hadn't offered his car because she had her own.

"No. I appreciate the offer, but no thanks. You take a cab over to my apartment and I'll drive you out to the plane."

Phil didn't kiss her goodbye at the airport, but Gilyan could see that he wanted to. It was surprising and somehow touching to see him unsure of himself. Finally, he took her hand. "All I can hope is," he said, "that you'll find yourself missing me!"

Gilyan smiled to herself as she drove back to

the apartment. Phil, usually so poised, was almost stammering as he left her.

Saturday night, Gilyan collected some notebooks, old press clippings, and a half-dozen sharpened pencils, and settled down at the small cherrywood desk in her room to outline her promotional campaign. Ardell was spending the weekend with the Daltons, friends who lived in Marin County.

Gilyan had been reading about Mrs. Darlinger, the opera's biggest sponsor, who had given official notice that she felt obliged to withdraw her support in the face of attendance apathy. Matt Groody was a great opera booster and this combination had given Gilyan an idea about Opera for Everyone—an opera that would appeal to the masses who liked good music but never considered attending the big dress affairs. If she could run a series of articles preceding each presentation—an interview with the conductor and leading performers, a story outline of each new production, then announcing a night's performance of Opera for Everyone with scaled-down tickets— she felt that such a campaign might draw in the masses. It might even draw Mrs. Darlinger back into the fold, as well as opera lovers who had stayed away because of the ticket price or the somewhat overwhelming emphasis on the elegantly gowned women who attended.

Gilyan worked on the campaign Saturday night and a good part of Sunday. By Monday morning, she felt she had a satisfactory outline on what she considered a topical idea. She would work each evening and, because of her promise to Hannah, tell Ardell that she was doing some writing on the side. Gilyan had long discussed trying her hand at a short story. Once she had the campaign in final format, she could approach Mrs. Darlinger. If Mrs. Darlinger sanctioned her idea, success would be assured.

That Monday, Julia Caldwell was optimistic. She had covered the Scanlon wedding on Saturday and felt she had done a good job. Her amber eyes glowed as she stuck her head into Gilyan's office. "Did Hannah say anything to you about my copy on the Scanlon wedding?" she asked.

"I haven't seen Hannah yet," Gilyan told her. "But I'll make it a point to tell you what she says."

"Elmer, bless his heart," Julia said, "read it when I gave it to him and liked it. He said Hannah passed it back to him without a single blue-pencil mark!"

Gilyan smiled. Elmer, at this point, would like whatever Julia wrote. "If Hannah let it go through as you wrote it, Julia, you had it right."

Later that afternoon, Hannah discussed the matter with Gilyan. "Julia did a very nice job on the Scanlon wedding," she said. "She's surprising me. I may have to eat my words."

"Perhaps you might want to reconsider, give Julia a chance to work into at least a part of your job. After all," Gilyan smiled, "it might take two of us to fill your shoes."

"If I have any choice in the matter, Gilyan, the job will be yours. I'm beginning to think Julia might work her way up into something better, but not so fast."

Before leaving for home, Gilyan made it a point to see Julia and tell her that Hannah thought her coverage of the wedding very well done.

At the apartment, Gilyan was astonished to find a letter from Rob Hunter. Eagerly, she tore the envelope open.

Rob somewhat dryly stated that he hadn't made the grade as a playwright, but was managing to keep his hand in, so to speak, by doing a bit of newspaper writing. He would enjoy hearing from her, how she liked working on the Woman's Page of the *Globe*.

Gilyan stopped reading for a moment. Rob had gone away before she got the job here. Apparently, Rob and her parents *had* kept in touch for him to know what she was doing. She went back to the letter. Rob said he planned to get out to the Coast in the not-too-distant future and hoped that they could get together and have one of their old-time sessions. He planned on seeing her mother and father at that time, too. If she got the chance, would she drop him a line?

Delighted, Gilyan sat right down and wrote to him. Before she knew it, she had told Rob all about her project. Smiling, she underlined the fact that the above was confidential. It reminded her of old times, when they would say to each other, "This is a secret, but I can tell you." They both knew they could trust each other. And Rob, also doing newspaper work, could tell her if the planned campaign sounded feasible. Rob might not have made it as a playwright, might not have had the necessary aggressive drive, but he *could* write.

Finally finished, Gilyan folded the thick sheets, put them into an envelope and stamped it; then she took the letter down to the corner box. She was already anticipating Rob's reply.

The next day, Gilyan came back into the office late, after covering a flower show. She typed up her notes, called Elmer, then went into Hannah's office.

"May I interrupt a minute, Hannah?"

Hannah raised a disheveled head. "Any time. How's everything coming along?" Hannah eyed Gilyan's burnt-orange suit. "You're mighty attractive in that color."

"Thank you. Hannah, my project is shaping up

beautifully. I think—hope—it will appear to Matt, too. It isn't finished, of course, but it won't be . . ." She broke off as Hannah looked over her shoulder, scowling. Gilyan turned to see Vida Barron in the doorway.

"Oh, Hannah," Vida drawled, "I'm leaving early. If anyone asks, tell them I have a head—ache." Vida gave Gilyan the ghost of a smile and disappeared from the doorway.

"Since when," Hannah said slowly, still scowling, "does Vida bother to tell me when she's leaving early? How long do you think she was standing there?"

Gilyan shook her head. "I don't know. However, I don't think for long, and I really hadn't said anything too . . ."

"I'm thinking about the other day," Hannah said. "Remember, when I first broached the subject to you in your office and had the idea someone was listening?" She shook her head and lit a fresh cigarette, and Gilyan automatically reached out to snuff the old one. "As I said then," Hannah went on, "I don't want Matt to know my plans until they're all in line—and that includes you. When you have the draft outline completed, bring it down. I'll go over it at my apartment."

"I should have the first draft ready for you to see by the week-end."

After a few more words with Hannah on her assignment for the next day, Gilyan left the building.

A wire came that night from Phil. He would be delayed in Miami for a few days, but would plane in the following Sunday. Could she meet him if he called her from the airport?

Ardell smiled as Gilyan gave her the gist of the message. "Have you missed him?" she asked.

Gilyan nodded. "Yes, I have. I've missed him a lot." But she didn't add that she couldn't analyze her feelings for Phil when she didn't know what her feelings might still be for Jay.

She found out on Saturday night.

Chapter Twelve

Saturday morning, Gilyan put her promotional campaign outline and notes into a large manila envelope to take down to Hannah. She would be glad to get them out of her room. Implying to Ardell that she was working on something else gave her a vague feeling of guilt. The moment Hannah gave her the go-ahead, she would tell Ardell all about the project and the reason for her secrecy.

Hannah was out when Gilyan reached the *Globe* office and, according to Julia, would be for most of the day. Hannah and Tom Monohan had gone down the Peninsula to cover the big Cartwright wedding and reception. Gilyan debated whether to take the manila envelope back to the apartment, but decided it would be safe enough locked in the middle drawer of her desk.

As she talked to Julia, Gilyan scrawled Hannah's name on the envelope. Elmer walked into the room and, as usual, his freckled face lit up when he saw Julia. "Mr. Groody wants to see you," he said.

Julia swallowed. "Me?" She turned to Gilyan. "Now what?" The slender face looked worried. "I can't imagine . . ."

Gilyan smiled reassuringly. "Remember last time? You were worried for nothing. Now run along and then come back in and we'll go over some of next week's events. I'll have some assignments for you." Gilyan was touched to see Julia's face brighten.

"I'll be right back," she said, and hurried out of the office.

Gilyan was sorting some of the engagement questionnaires when a voice said, "May I come in?" She looked up, and was surprised to see Vida.

There was something subtly different about Vida. Usually, her beauty lay in the superficial vividness of the red mouth and white skin under blue-black hair, like some one-dimensional, boldly stroked painting that lacked depth and warmth. Today, the painting had come alive, even to the blue-green eyes; their glow was softer, warmer. Gilyan found, almost immediately, that happiness had achieved this high-lighted effect.

"May I talk to you a minute?" The drawl wasn't so pronounced, the tone gentler. As Gilyan nodded, Vida sat down.

Gilyan offered her a cigarette, then looked questioningly at Vida. Vida smiled and Gilyan sucked in her breath. The difference was astonishing. This smile reached the blue-green eyes, and for the first time, Gilyan saw an animation that gave Vida's face a radiant beauty.

"It seems to me," Vida said quietly, "that every female should have someone with whom to share happy news." The smile twisted the least bit. "Due to my unfortunate disposition, there are few people who would be interested in any news concerning me—especially happy news."

"I wouldn't say that," Gilyan cut in, suddenly very sorry for the girl across from her.

Vida shrugged. "I've asked for it. However, you're different. I want you to know." A delicate tint came into the ivory cheeks. "It looks like Tom . . . Well, perhaps my being such a good crying towel has paid off."

Gilyan leaned forward. "Vida, I'm so glad!"

Vida nodded. "I knew you would be. I guess he's over Julia." A slight frown puckered the smooth brows. "I noticed the past weeks he'd stopped mentioning her and I was afraid to question this. Then, the other night, when he said something," the delicate tint in her cheeks deepened, "I finally became brave enough to ask about his feelings for Julia." Vida's frown deepened. "He just scowled and snapped something to the effect that the competition there was too rich for his blood, that he wouldn't buck that kind of competition if she was the last girl in California."

Gilyan was bewildered. "Competition? What on earth did he mean?"

Vida shook her head and gave a rueful laugh. "I wasn't about to ask him. The net result of how he feels now is quite enough for me. Anyway," she added in a burst of candor, "there was an angry look on his face that told me it was no time to ask questions." She leaned forward. "In the past weeks, Tom's actions have told me plainer than words that he is beginning to like me. I wouldn't say or do anything to jeopardize that."

Gilyan suddenly understood. "In other words," she said slowly, "you think Tom might be mistaken but are afraid to correct his error in judgment?"

"That's right. This office is a veritable grapevine and I've never heard anything about Julia having a boy friend. With the cloistered life she leads, I don't see how she could have one. And where Tom might have heard such a thing, I can't remotely imagine. Am I doing wrong in not arguing the point?" The red mouth looked mutinous. "Julia has never indicated the least interest in Tom, and heaven knows he's done everything but stand on his head to attract her attention. Now, he's definitely showing that his feelings for me are undergoing a change. Should I jeopardize that by

130

going to bat for a girl whom I barely know? To whom I owe nothing and from whom I'm taking nothing she wants?"

Gilyan shook her head. "I don't think you should be expected to go that far. However, I do think Tom's wrong. If Tom's becoming interested in you, that is fine. But if he says something concrete that you can refute, I think that only fair, too. To Julia."

Vida's eye met Gilyan's in a clear stare. "The few times he's mentioned this, he's sounded very bitter, almost as though outraged by the fact that someone wasn't what he thought them. Now, he never mentions Julia. But if he does say something, something that can be refuted, I'll come and tell you and let you do what you think best. All right?"

Gilyan nodded. "Of course. And Vida," she smiled, "I'm really delighted that things are turning out for you."

Vida rose. "Tom's practically stopped drinking. Isn't that wonderful?" Her eyes fell on the manila envelope on Gilyan's desk. "D'you need some stamps, or do you want me to give that to Elmer?"

Casually, Gilyan picked up the envelope. "Oh no, thanks. Just some notes I have for Hannah."

Gilyan's mind was spinning. What could Tom Monahan have meant by saying that Julia's competition was too rich for his blood? That even if he could, he wouldn't buck *that* kind of competition?

The object of her thoughts suddenly stuck her blonde head inside the door. The amber eyes were dancing.

"Mr. Groody congratulated me on the Scanlon assignment!"

Gilyan smiled at the lovely, eager face. "Good. Did Hannah show it to him?"

Julia nodded. "I guess so. I'm going to have to stop being frightened every time Mr. Groody calls me into the office. I'm a little in awe of him, I guess." She laughed. "He does have quite a bark —even when he's trying to be pleasant!"

Gilyan smiled back. "I know." Even as she was talking, she was trying to think of a way to probe into what could have caused Tom Monahan's abrupt change of attitude toward the girl before her. Suddenly, she recalled that day at lunch when Julia had told her that she was going steady with someone and she had thought that Julia was lying. Perhaps Julia had told Tom something along that line. Julia was obviously a gentle person and would hate hurting him. Yet, even so, why would the competition be too rich for his blood? This denoted wealth. And he wouldn't buck this competition if Julia was the last girl in the state, which denoted disapproval.

Julia's voice broke into her thoughts.

"I thought surely you would notice this one." She was indicating the soft apricot wool sheath she wore. On one shoulder was a striking crescent of dull gold set with topazes.

"I did notice it!" Gilyan exclaimed. "I was just going to mention it when Elmer said Matt wanted to see you. Turn around—it's perfectly beautiful."

Julia turned slowly, arms out, mannequin-like. "Isn't the fit perfect? And look at the pin? When I opened the box I was so thrilled . . ."

Julia was so manifestly happy that Gilyan wouldn't have spoiled her mood with questions if she had been able to find the right ones to ask. Vida could have misunderstood Tom, or Tom could have misunderstood something he heard from Julia or another source. Better, right now, to let the matter remain dormant. As Vida said, she wasn't taking anything from Julia. If Julia had wanted Tom, she could have had him.

"Let's have a cup of coffee," Gilyan said to Julia. She picked up the manila envelope and slipped a big metal clip on the outside, then locked it in the middle drawer of her desk.

That night after dinner, Gilyan showered and changed into a lounging suit of blue silk that her father had brought her from Hong Kong. She caught back the heavy copper hair with a band of black velvet, then padded, in brocaded black slippers, into the living room for a quiet evening of reading.

Ardell was dressing to go over to the Daltons' in Marin County. When she came into the living room, ready to go, Gilyan told her now nice she looked in her new green coat.

"It's so nice to be going to your own shower!" Ardell laughed. "Even though it *is* a surprise shower. When Marge called last week, she said—'You be sure and be here Monday night, because it's a surprise, post-married shower for you.'" Ardell looked at Gilyan. "Sure you don't want to come? They'd love having you."

Gilyan shook her head. "The Daltons don't even know me. And I'll get in on another shower for you."

"That's good," Ardell said complacently. "Newlyweds can use a lot of loot!" Laughing, she went out the door.

The door had been closed only a few minutes when the downstairs buzzer sounded and Gilyan thought Ardell must have forgotten something and left her key. Carrying her magazine, she walked into the small foyer and pressed the door release, then stood waiting by the hall door. When the hall buzzer sounded, she threw open the door, saying, "What did you forget—?"

The words froze in her throat, and Gilyan had to hold tightly to the door. Jay was standing in the hallway, staring down at her.

"May I come in, please?" he finally asked, the dark eyes intent on her.

Slowly, Gilyan released the doorknob and stepped back, feeling at a disadvantage in the informality of the silk lounging suit, the Alice-in-Wonderland hairdo.

Jay was shrugging out of his brown topcoat and laying it and his hat on the foyer stand. He walked into the yellow living room and turned, waiting.

Gilyan braced herself for a rush of feeling at seeing him again in the familiar setting—the many nights when he had come in, his overcoat beaded with fog, and putting it down on the foyer stand to turn and take her into his arms.

The rush of feeling failed to materialize. Gilyan thought perhaps she was slightly stunned; delayed shock was permitting the numbness. Slowly, she walked forward and sat down. She couldn't understand her immediate reaction—or lack of it. The deeply tanned face with its smooth planes and angles, the lowered dark brows over dark eyes were the features of some acquaintance, a person she knew out of the past. It couldn't possibly be that this could be resolved so simply. In a moment now, a rush of emotion would grip her by the throat.

"I had to talk to you." Jay sat down facing her. He was nervous. "I wouldn't have blamed you in the least if you had closed the door in my face."

Still, no feeling. "What did you want to say?" Gilyan's voice was even.

For a moment, a look of something like dismay

flickered in the dark eyes. Or was it surprise? "You know, of course, there are many things that should be said to you, Gilyan. My behavior was inexcusable, yet there *were* mitigating circumstances."

Gilyan was still trying to understand her reaction, suspicious of it, waiting for the pain to recur. "Were there mitigating circumstances?" she asked.

Jay nodded. "You would have to know Nancy Covington to really understand, Gilyan. She—she is an overwhelming person. From the moment we met . . . Then, there was drinking . . . I—I didn't stand a chance in company like that!"

"In other words," Gilyan's words sounded clipped, "she took advantage of your naïveté?"

A slow red swept over his face. "I deserved that. But yes, if you like. I'm not used to running into such fast company. With Nancy and her crowd, it's anything they want to do and when they want to do it."

"Was Nancy's crowd with her when you met on the plane?" Gilyan asked, feeling that some interest must be drawn on her period of indignity and pain.

The red deepened. "Of course not. When we met on the plane she was alone. For some strange reason, she took a liking to me. Everywhere I turned in New York, there was Nancy. This sounds lousy to say, but she forced the issue."

"If that's the case, why did *she* leave you?"

For a moment, he looked taken aback. Then he stammered, "As I've tried to show you, Gilyan, that's the way she is—her whole crowd is. If they want something, they proceed to get it. Then they find they don't want it." He cleared his throat. "Their feelings don't go very deep."

Disgust rose in Gilyan. "Do yours? You know, Jay, I could find a lot more excuse for you if you'd been swept off your feet by Nancy Covington. But to say you meekly let yourself be led to the altar by some girl who just happened to have taken a fancy to you! I can't buy that."

Jay's mouth tightened. "Talk about feelings not going very deep! What about yours? I've heard about you and that Dr. Randall. You managed to get over me pretty fast!"

"I have no reason to explain anything to you but, just to set the record straight, Phil Randall is only a friend."

Suddenly, Jay left the couch and knelt beside Gilyan, folding his arms around the blue silk shoulders. His mouth came down on hers—and it was the best thing that could have happened. The feeling that she had had for him was dead. Quite dead. Passively, she waited until he drew back. He stared, then slowly backed to the couch and sat down again. Gilyan could see the fury mounting in him.

"So . . . It isn't the doctor? Then who? That

Lamplighter fellow? I might've known. He thought he was being so cagey! And *you* talk about my depth of feeling . . ."

Gilyan was staring speechlessly, her mind trying to make sense of the words Jay was hurling at her. Finally, she managed, "Jay! What under the sun are you *talking* about? What Lamplighter fellow?"

"What Lamplighter fellow!" Jay's mouth twisted. "Don't pull the innocent act with me. I noticed how he came down off his high horse the minute I mentioned knowing you!"

Gilyan's own temper rose to meet his. "Will you please stop ranting and tell me what you're talking about?"

"That columnist!" he shouted. "The Lamplighter! *Rob Hunter!* The great white light of Broadway's night life!"

For a long moment, Gilyan continued to stare, her mind a jumble of confusion. How could Rob Hunter be The Lamplighter? "Oh, no!" she finally gasped.

"Oh, yes!" Jay sneered. "He told me—once he deigned to notice me after I mentioned you—that you'd been childhood friends, and then he asked some thousand questions about you."

So that was when he wrote . . . "If, as you say, he asked a thousand questions about me, you should know we haven't seen each other for a long time." Why was she bothering to explain anything to Jay?

"I thought," Jay said bitterly, "that you meant it when you said you loved me."

"That just goes to show how wrong a person—*two* persons—can be about an emotion. Now," she rose, "if you'll excuse me?"

He walked stiffly to the foyer and shrugged into his topcoat, then looked back at her. "I thought that you, Gilyan, were fair-minded enough to give a person another chance. "You would," he said accusingly, "if you *really* cared for me."

Gilyan's hazel eyes stared back at him from across the room. "I would, Jay, if I really cared for you."

Gilyan's mind seemed wound tight when she climbed into bed. Rob—The Lamplighter! Why hadn't someone told her? Her parents, or Rob himself? It was obvious that her parents knew, so it followed that, for some reason, Rob didn't want her to know. Perhaps he intended to surprise her with the news when he came out to San Francisco on his business trip. As her mind slowed, a wave of thankfulness caught her. She was cured of Jay. She need no longer fear seeing him. Would this make any difference in her relationship with Phil Randall? He had been wonderfully patient . . .

Chapter Thirteen

Sunday night, waiting for Phil Randall's plane to land, Gilyan recalled Ardell's reaction to the news that Rob Hunter was The Lamplighter.

Round-eyed, Ardell had exclaimed, "And you said Rob Hunter wasn't sophisticated enough for you?" She shook the flyaway blonde hair. "He writes the most sophisticated satire I've ever read! Did you know that Matt plans to carry his column in the *Globe?*"

Strangely nettled, Gilyan nodded, and was relieved when Ardell changed the subject, reverting to Jay and how happy she was that Gilyan seemed completely over him. Then Ardell asked, "You'll tell Phil, won't you? He deserves a clear field."

Slowly, Gilyan nodded. "Yes, he deserves to know. And I'm as relieved as you are to find that Jay no longer has the power to hurt me."

As Gilyan stood by the gate to the airport, she turned her head and saw a woman standing a few feet away. For a long moment, Gilyan didn't realize that the woman was Alice Groody. She looked ill, and had lost a lot of weight. There were heavy circles under the light-blue eyes. A man was just walking away from her and Alice was folding a thin sheaf of papers and putting them in her purse. As she turned, Gilyan walked over to her.

"Alice!" She bit back words of shock as the gaunt face lifted to hers. "I—I haven't seen you for such a long time."

Dully, Alice shook her head. "It has been a long time, hasn't it? How have you been, Gilyan? How are your folks?" Alice seemed to be feverishly snatching words out of the air.

Gilyan told Alice that she was fine and that her folks would be back, for good, shortly. Then, because the ravaged look was so marked, Gilyan gently added, "Alice, have you been ill?"

The plain face under the mousey brown hair didn't change expression. "Ill? Oh, no. I've been working pretty hard on this committee and that." She smiled vaguely. "Perhaps I've lost some weight." Almost disinterestedly, she glanced down at the loose suit. "Yes, I guess I have." She looked up. "Are you meeting someone?"

Gilyan nodded. "A friend of mine is coming in from Miami." Alice Groody didn't volunteer what she was doing at the airport, and Gilyan didn't ask. The ill-looking woman reached out and gave Gilyan's hand a pat, then walked away, toward the big waiting room.

Gilyan didn't have time to think about the change in Alice Groody as the Miami ship turned downwind and touched onto the runway. Phil Randall was among the first passengers to get off. His eyes lighted up as he saw her, and somewhat shyly, Gilyan leaned forward and touched his cheek with her lips.

"Well," he looked surprised, "that makes for a very nice welcome." He laughed and added, "I'll bet you know I have a present tucked away in my pocket for you."

"That's right," Gilyan said placidly. "I always kiss gentlemen bearing gifts."

They decided to have dinner at the airport restaurant, and over coffee, Gilyan, suddenly distressingly tongue-tied, tried to introduce the subject of Jay and her change of feeling toward him. She managed to get out the fact that Jay had come to her apartment the night before, and Phil misunderstood.

Quickly, he leaned across the small table and put one warm hand on hers. "Ah, Gilyan! That must have been very hard for you—seeing him again. I can imagine how you're feeling. It was sweet of you to come to meet me under the circumstances." His dark eyes were full of concern.

Gilyan laughed, and a startled expression swept

across Phil's face. "You don't understand what I'm trying to tell you," she said. "His coming by the apartment last night was the best thing he could have done! Doctor, this patient is cured!"

"Cured?" Phil looked bewildered. "Cured?"

"Yes." Gilyan nodded. "Apparently what I felt for Jay wasn't the real thing, or his actions killed my feeling for him."

"I see . . ." Phil said slowly, and Gilyan waited expectantly for him to say something more. His sudden stillness, the expression on his face, seemed strange to Gilyan; she had a feeling of rebuff. "I see," he said again, and drawing back his hand, he shook a cigarette loose in the package lying on the table and offered one to her.

Automatically, Gilyan took the cigarette. Try as she might, she couldn't read Phil's expression. Disapproving? Was Phil thinking that she was shallow?

This reaction on his part was the last thing she had expected. His past actions had led her to believe that there would be some measure of rejoicing on his part when and if he learned there was a clear field.

Gilyan's discomfiture was heightened when Phil changed the subject. He talked about Miami as they finished their coffee and continued on the subject during their drive back to Gilyan's apartment. He was tired, he couldn't come in, but he would call Gilyan during the week and make a date.

Ardell was surprised to see her back so early.

"Well," she looked up eagerly, "did you tell Phil about Jay coming over and your reaction to him?"

"I did," Gilyan said, almost in tears, "and I wish to heaven I had the past hour to live over so that I could unsay it!"

Ardell dropped her feet from the hassock and sat up straight. "What do you mean? Here . . ." she said, as Gilyan continued to stand stiffly by the door, "sit down."

Gilyan crossed the room, removing the bulky tweed knit cardigan she wore over her gray sheath. "I mean I wish I hadn't told Phil I was over Jay. I—I feel embarrassed! I—I feel . . . I don't know *how* I feel!" she exclaimed, sitting down and looking almost pleadingly at Ardell.

Her roommate shook her head. "Now, wait a minute. Go over it all, so that I'll know what you're talking about."

Gilyan sank back, her eyes on the far wall. "I told Phil that Jay had come by the apartment last night. At first," a frown furrowed the smooth forehead under the coppery hair, "he was warm and sympathetic. He misunderstood, thought the visit had upset me. Then I corrected him. I told him that Jay's visit was the best thing that could have happened, that I was cured, that apparently what

I thought for Jay wasn't the real thing—or his actions had killed my feeling for him . . ."

Ardell was leaning intently forward, a question in her eyes.

Gilyan shrugged. "He seemed to withdraw. He said, 'I see,' then handed me a cigarette and changed the subject." Gilyan's cheeks were scarlet as she relived the moment.

"Oh, Gilyan! What did you expect? Phil has been so patient during this time he knew you cared for someone else that he's just become overly wary. Wary of being hurt, wary of your change toward Jay. Do you think he would want to get hurt? I imagine he has a lot of pride and has done quite a bit of swallowing of that pride since he met you."

Slowly, the clouded look lifted from Gilyan's face. "Do you think so, Ardell? Do you think that could be it?"

"Of course I do. What did you think his reaction meant?"

Gilyan flushed. "I was afraid he thought I was being as shallow as Jay."

Ardell hooted. "He knows you better than that. It's obvious now that you were in love with someone who didn't exist. You can't stay in love with a reasonable facsimile of something. Another thing —did you give Phil the slightest indication that you cared for him?"

Gilyan shook her head. "No, of course not. It

wouldn't be true in that sense. This isn't a case of off with the old and on with the new. But he's been so considerate, so kind and patient, I didn't say I *couldn't* come to care for him . . ."

"There you are!" Ardell pounced triumphantly. "He senses that and realizes that he must continue to move very slowly indeed."

And because Gilyan wanted Ardell's explanation to be the right one, she let herself be convinced. In the very beginning, Phil had told her that he was in love with her and his patience, consideration, and constant attendance since certainly verified this feeling of his. Gilyan had been too abrupt. Such news would take time to digest.

In bed, Gilyan forced her mind to other channels. It would be strange to have Rob Hunter—in a sense—working for the same paper when and if Matt carried his column. Gilyan finally slept and dreamed that Rob, carrying a lamp, walked into her office and told her he was sorry but the *Globe* was dispensing with her services, that her writing lacked sophistication.

Chapter Fourteen

Monday was hectic at the *Globe*. Hannah had had an infected wisdom tooth extracted late Saturday and wouldn't be in for a few days. Talking was an obvious effort so Gilyan didn't prolong their telephone conversation. She just told Hannah to take care of herself and come back when she felt all right, that she and Julia would manage. Gilyan never gave a thought to the manila envelope locked away in her desk drawer.

Phil didn't call until Tuesday night, and only then to tell Gilyan he very much doubted if he would be able to see her before the first of the following week. Work had accumulated during his time away. Gilyan found nothing wrong with his words or tone, but hung up again feeling the sense of chill, of rebuff.

Vida, still with the new glow, come into Gilyan's office Thursday morning. And once again, she gave her a shock; this time, without barb or intent.

Tom had taken Vida to Theatre-in-the-Round, the night before. "Tom," Vida said, "was working, of course, but I thoroughly enjoyed myself. He kept drifting off, during intermission, to take pictures of the opening night audience, but he warned me before we left that he had to do this." The blue-green eyes were shining. "Saturday night, he's taking me out to dinner and a show."

Gilyan was pleased. "I'm so glad," she said. "By the way," she added tentatively, "has he said anything more about Julia?"

Vida shook her head. "Not a word. In fact," the red lips curved upward, "he doesn't mention her any more. I'm not pressing my luck." She turned to go, and threw her innocent bombshell. "Didn't you used to go out with a Dr. Randall?"

Gilyan nodded. "Yes. Phil Randall. Do you know him?"

"No. But I heard Ardell talking with you about him one day in the lounge, and I saw him pick you up once. I saw him last night. He sat two rows in front of us at the Theatre-in-the-Round. The girl with him had on one of those hair-concealing hats and I thought it was you; as we got up for intermission, I leaned forward and tapped her on the shoulder. She and Dr. Randall turned around and gave me perfectly blank stares." Vida flushed. "I was slightly embarrassed."

Gilyan didn't change expression. "I've done that myself," she said, "so I know how you felt."

She was still sitting, frozen, when Ardell came in. Ardell stopped. "What's the matter?"

Gilyan said, "Vida saw Phil at Theatre-in-the-Round last night, with a date."

"I don't believe it!" Ardell snapped. "I wouldn't believe Vida under oath."

Gilyan shook her head. "Vida didn't tell me with the intention of hurting me. She told me without knowing that I still go out with Phil."

"Maybe it was a colleague's wife, or a relative," Ardell said.

"And maybe it wasn't." Gilyan's hazel eyes met Ardell's. "He told me when he called on Tuesday night that accumulated work would keep him busy all week."

Phil didn't call over the week-end. And Monday morning, Hannah was back and Gilyan was kept busy filling her in on assignments covered and those to be covered. She told Hannah she had the folder on her project locked in her desk drawer and would show it to her whenever Hannah was ready.

"Good!" Hannah had lost some of her color

during the week and still talked as though her jaw hurt. "Is it all complete?"

Gilyan, wanting to get a sanction from Mrs. Darlinger, shook her head. "There's someone I want to see, someone who, if I can get her approval, should automatically put Matt's seal of approval on the whole thing."

Hannah looked questioning, then nodded. "I trust your judgment, Gilyan. Go ahead with your final step, then bring the whole thing into me." The fact that Gilyan hadn't mentioned the subject of her project never occurred to her at the time.

Gilyan went into Julia's little cubbyhole. "Julia, do you have Mrs. Darlinger's address and telephone number in your social files?"

Julia walked to a big file. "I certainly do." She smiled, then hesitated. "You know she's still in Europe, don't you?"

Gilyan tried to hide her disappointment. "Oh, is she?"

"Yes. She won't be back for a couple of weeks."

"Darn! Well," Gilyan shrugged, "maybe when I get back I can see her."

Julia looked surprised. "Are you going away?"

Gilyan nodded. "The folks get back from London next week-end so I'm taking a week of my vacation and going up there."

"I'll miss you," Julia said.

Gilyan smiled at the small blonde girl and went

back to her desk. She was glad to be busy. Perhaps Phil would call tonight.

But there was no call that night.

Tuesday morning, Gilyan brought the final notes on her project down to her office to put into the manila folder. When she unlocked the middle desk drawer, she stared. Hadn't she put a clip, a big clip, on the folder? There certainly was none there now. Swiftly, she leafed through the neatly typed pages. They were intact. She must have imagined the clip. She attached the addenda and relocked the drawer. Perhaps when she returned from her week in Oregon, Mrs. Darlinger would be back, and she would have the project completed, and sanctioned, for Hannah's okay before taking it on to Matt. There was little doubt that if Gilyan could sell Mrs. Darlinger on the idea Matt would go all out for the Opera for Everyone campaign.

Late Wednesday afternoon, Gilyan had two telephone calls. One was from her father in New York verifying their return on Saturday and her coming up to Oregon the following week. The second call was from Sandra Haviland, asking Gilyan if they could have dinner together on Thursday night. Bill was out of town, Sandra said, and she didn't like dining alone. Pleased, Gilyan accepted. Perhaps Sandra, knowing Phil so well, could dissolve some of the fog of bewilderment surrounding Gilyan.

Gilyan met Sandra Thursday evening, and almost immediately Sandra supplied the key to the puzzle. The slender blonde woman, elegant in chalk-white that accentuated her smooth tan, clasped Gilyan's hand.

"Where," she exclaimed, eyeing Gilyan's smart brown flannel suit and burnt-orange feathered hat, "do you get your clothes? Your color combinations are right out of this world."

Pleased, Gilyan settled herself across the candlelit table. "My mother has an eye for materials and buys a lot of things for me in England and Scotland. She has an excellent dressmaker and all I have to do, really, is add the accessories."

"Which," Sandra said dryly, "have made or broken many an expensive outfit. You have a definite flair."

They ordered, and Sandra lit a cigarette, looking across the flaring match at Gilyan. "Have you seen Phil lately?" she asked.

Gilyan shook her head. "I haven't seen him since I met his plane, a week ago, Sunday night."

"Isn't that rather unusual?" Sandra asked lightly.

"He called a week ago Tuesday and said work had accumulated during his time away in Miami." Gilyan didn't mention Vida's having seen him with another girl at Theatre-in-theRound. Phil and Sandra were old friends and Sandra might not like an implied criticism of an old friend. Gilyan was wrong.

The blue eyes in the tanned face across from her narrowed. "I'm forever sounding like Susie-Pry when I talk to you, but my intentions are the best, Gilyan. Did anything happen that Sunday night when you met Phil at the plane?"

Gilyan, still not feeling free to discuss Phil with an old friend of his, hedged. "Anything happen? What do you mean?"

"Well, speaking about as frankly as one can, I mean did you by chance change your feeling toward Phil and let him know?"

There was an undercurrent here that she didn't understand. Gilyan shook her head. "No."

Sandra looked astonished. "You didn't? I would have bet on it!" she cried. "Don't tell me I'm wrong this time . . ." Sandra added, sounding as if she were talking to herself.

Further bewildered, Gilyan stared. "I—I don't follow you."

Their waiter arrived at this point and she and Sandra sat silently while he served them, then Sandra leaned forward.

"Gilyan, why did you tell Phil you couldn't come over Sunday night? To our place—that is."

"Which Sunday?" Gilyan's tone was blank.

"Last Sunday."

"Phil didn't ask me out last Sunday. The last

time I talked to him was a week ago Tuesday, and he only called then to tell me he was busy. I didn't know anything about going to your place."

"So!" Sandra looked triumphant. "I thought so! Now think, carefully. What did you say to Phil the night you met his plane . . . Wait!" A thoughtful look crossed Sandra's face. "What about that newspaper fellow you care for? Has anything happened there?"

Without having intended to, Gilyan was suddenly telling Sandra in detail about Jay's visit to her apartment and how, to her relief, she found she no longer cared for him. How, over dinner at the airport restaurant, she had told this to Phil—and Phil's somewhat chilling reaction. Sandra was emphatically nodding her head, tightening her mouth.

"Exactly. The old familiar pattern right down the line, and Bill and I had been so in hopes he had changed." As Gilyan stared, forgetting the cooling food on her plate, Sandra explained.

"Haven't you ever wondered why Phil isn't married? Nice looking, certainly at—or past—the marriageable age, definitely eligible? Well, I'll tell you why." The blue eyes chilled. "Phil's a *pursuer*. I don't think Phil will ever marry. I can cite three separate instances. Nice girls. He's quite a Don Juan, our Phil. Considerate and attentive but—and this is a Lulu of a but—once he has them emotionally snagged, our boy promptly loses interest. He goes kiting off like the string's been cut in a high wind. It's my opinion," Sandra's tone was biting, "that the good Dr. Randall should see a psychiatrist!" Quickly, she added, "Don't get me wrong. Phil's been a friend of Bill's and mine for years. As a friend—he's fine. But heaven deliver me from him as a suitor!"

Gilyan felt exactly like someone being told white was black. "Why—why—" she finally managed, "you can't be right. I didn't tell him I cared for him!"

"I know, I know," Sandra said tersely. "But the potential was there. Here Phil has been pursuing a girl who was quite disinterested. Her interest was in another man. Phil was in his element. Then the girl tells him the other man is out of the picture. What would logically evolve? Wouldn't the girl quite naturally turn to the man who had been so considerate during the girl's unhappy state over another man?"

Sandra saw the open disbelief in Gilyan's face. "I can imagine how hard this is to understand. I know Phil. But at least you're prepared." She looked down at Gilyan's plate. "Oh, fine. I've ruined your dinner, and left you unconvinced— which shows you have a nice sense of loyalty— and all I wanted was to do you a good turn. We won't discuss this further, and I just hope you don't thoroughly dislike me now."

Gilyan shook her head and slowly picked up

her fork. "Of course I don't dislike you for trying to do me a favor. I—I guess I just need time to think about this. As you say, it's hard to comprehend."

Friday seemed an unbearably long day. Late in the afternoon, Julia came to her door looking pale and wan. "I'm sorry, Gilyan," she said faintly, "but I'm afraid I'll have to go home. My head hurts dreadfully and I feel all achy as if I'm coming down with the flu."

Gilyan made Julia sit down while she got her an aspirin, then called a cab for her.

Saturday morning, Gilyan reached the *Globe* office to find an excited cluster around her doorway and the acrid smell of burned, wet wood in the air. The group at the door parted to let her through, and she looked in dismay on the wreck that was her office. Her desk and the wall behind it were charcoal. The wastebasket, a blackened ruin, was tipped on its side. Water stood in great puddles over the floor.

"What happened?" Gilyan turned to Ardell.

"Isn't it a mess?" Ardell dropped her voice. "I called the apartment as soon as I got here, but you were gone. Somebody must have emptied an ash tray into the wastebasket with a live coal in it. The door was shut and no one noticed the smoldering fire until it had gone up the side of your desk from the wastebasket. Thank heaven it didn't get to your files."

Something Ardell had just said struck a discordant chord in Gilyan's mind, something off key, but at the moment she was too appalled to think clearly. Her desk and everything on it was a soaking, blackened mess. Fire had eaten right up the side and across the top. Gilyan suddenly remembered her project and ran forward. The whole front of the desk, including the middle and side drawers, was destroyed.

Elmer was standing on the edge of the staring people. "Elmer," Gilyan turned to him, "what time did you get here?"

Elmer flushed. "Early, but I didn't know you had a fire in here. Your door was closed." Surprisingly, he sounded almost belligerent; then he ducked his head and darted off.

It was then that the off-key thought clicked into place. Gilyan had left her door open as she always had. She definitely recalled going into Hannah's office with a heavy file in her arms just before leaving the building, and the door was wide open at that time. The cleaning women always left it that way. Why was it closed last night? Gilyan didn't have much time to worry about the matter.

Julia called in, still ill, and Gilyan moved into Julia's office for the rest of the day, which involved a lot of carrying back and forth from her files. Matt didn't seem particularly perturbed.

"We're insured," he said. "We'll have it all cleaned up by the time you get back from your week off. You'll get a new desk."

Gilyan wasn't worried about getting a new desk; she was worried about the destroyed contents of the one she had had. Her whole promotional campaign had gone up in smoke. When she had a moment to herself, she tried to visualize what might have happened. Was Hannah in her office just before they left for the day? Hannah constantly left still-burning cigarettes on the rim of an ash tray while she lighted another. Had that happened yesterday?

When Hannah came in, she, too, felt bad about Gilyan's project. "That's a dirty shame!" she exclaimed. "Do you think you'll be able to work from your original copy?"

Gilyan looked shamefaced. "Once I completed the project, I destroyed my notes," she said. "I know it was foolish," she added at the astonished look on Hannah's face. "But you had asked me not to mention the project until you'd given Matt notice—so I was working rather secretively at the apartment. When I brought the completed project down here, I locked it in the desk and threw the rough draft away." Gilyan's face brightened. "Look. I'll have a week at home and can get started again while it's fresh in my mind."

Hannah looked half-relieved, half-concerned.

"That seems rather mean—having you work on your vacation."

Gilyan was firm. "If I was careless enough to toss a burning coal into my wastebasket—and foolish enough to tear up my notes—I deserve having to work on my vacation."

As Gilyan said goodbye to the switchboard girl that evening, she suddenly remembered that she wouldn't get a chance to say goodbye to Julia. "Marie," she asked the switchboard operator, "do you have Julia Caldwell's address?" Marie gave her a number on Vista Street and Gilyan wrote it down on a slip of paper and left.

She stopped at a bookstore and picked out a current best seller that she thought Julia might like. Gilyan wouldn't go upstairs, at the Vista Street address, but would put a note in the book and leave it with Julia's apartment manager.

She hailed a taxi and gave the address on Vista, then sat back and penned a note. She told Julia about the fire and that she had used her office, making it light, then said she hoped she would be feeling much better soon. Gilyan inserted the note in the front of the book and put the book back into the green and white bag. The taxi was pulling to a halt and stopping.

Gilyan looked out, then frowned. They were in a block of very swank, towering apartments and apartment-hotels. "Are you sure you came to the right number?" Gilyan asked blankly.

"It's the one you gave me, lady," the taxi driver stated.

Gilyan looked at the slip of paper in her hand, then up to the white number painted on the gray awning that crossed the sidewalk. "Just a moment," she said. "Wait for me."

She went into a softly elegant foyer of muted rose and gray. The man at the desk looked up.

"May I help you?" he asked.

Gilyan cleared her throat. This was idiotic, really. She had the wrong address, of course. "I'm looking for the apartment of a Miss Julia Caldwell."

The man's white-maned head shook. "I'm sorry. We have no Miss Julia Caldwell here."

Gilyan thanked him and left. Well, she wouldn't have time now to try Marie again for the correct address. Her watch showed six, she hadn't had dinner, and she wanted to call Phil. She climbed into the cab and gave her California Street address.

There was a note for Gilyan at the apartment from Ardell, saying she was eating out and going to a show. A nice bit of tact. Ardell knew Gilyan planned to call Phil and ask him if he would drop by for a few minutes.

Gilyan dreaded the call. She forced herself to prepare and swallow some food; then she showered and changed into a silvery-gray crepe that always made her feel at her best. She slipped gray suede pumps on her feet and clasped the heavy amethyst choker and bracelet about her neck and wrist. With a final touch to the shining wings of coppery hair, Gilyan took a deep breath and walked to the telephone. As the number started to ring, she found herself half-hoping he would be out. He wasn't.

The moment his hello came over the wire, Gilyan found a knot in her throat. "Phil," she finally managed uncomfortably, "this is Gilyan."

"Oh, yes—Gilyan. How are you? I've been meaning to call," he continued politely, "but that trip to Florida really backed up my work."

"I'm sure it did," Gilyan managed, equally polite; then she plunged. "Phil, this is Saturday, so you probably have plans. However, I'm leaving tomorrow for Oregon, and I wonder if you'd drop by for a few moments."

Dismayed, Gilyan sensed his reluctance. "I assure you it won't take more than fifteen minutes," she said.

His capitulation was sudden. "Very well. But it will have to be short. I have an appointment at nine."

During the twenty-five minute wait, Gilyan paced the floor. When Phil reached the apartment, he was smiling.

"Ah, Gilyan," he said, "it's nice to see you. You're looking lovely." The words sounded like rote to her sensitive ear.

They sat down and, without preamble, Gilyan began: "Phil, is something wrong? I always thought we were very good friends."

Uncomfortably, he looked down at the hands clasped loosely in front of him. "Gilyan—" he cleared his throat, "this is hard for a man to do, but—well, if you must know, I think I was a bit precipitate in telling you I cared for you. Don't get me wrong." He raised his head, looking across at her. "I admire you very much. You're a lovely and intelligent person, but under the circumstances, I thought it might be best if I didn't see you for a while."

"I see." Gilyan wasn't going to help him. Anger stirred deeply within her.

"Yes." Again, he looked down at his hands. "You see, I spoke impulsively. You're," his look flattered her, "a very beautiful person and I really did think—there in the beginning—that I was in —well, in love with you." His expression brightened suddenly. "But I don't think you really care for me. It's just that . . ."

"I," said Gilyan levelly, "have never intimated by word or look that I care for you."

The brown eyes looked startled. "Oh . . . I see."

Gilyan stood up. "I think that covers it, Phil. You'd better leave for your business appointment."

For a moment, Gilyan actually thought he was going to do an about-face. His look softened and he took a step toward her, then, perhaps at the inflexible expression on her face, he turned quietly and walked out the door.

As Gilyan stood facing the closing door, a feeling of depression swept over her. Perhaps she could have cared for Phil Randall. Face it. If so, what did that make her? As shallow a person as Phil and Jay? Was there something wrong—some inner lack—within herself that made her attract, or become attracted to, unstable men?

When Ardell came in, Gilyan told her exactly what had happened. "Maybe," she said bitterly, "the same results apply when you cast other than bread on the water!"

"What do you mean?" Ardell asked, still smarting under the knowledge that she had misjudged Phil so completely.

Gilyan shrugged, turned back to the vanity mirror and pulled the brush through her hair. "Cast a frost on the waters and you yourself might do a bit of freezing. Perhaps I'm getting back what I gave Rob." Gilyan's chin shook and she firmed it. "Or perhaps I'm just not the type to arouse a lasting feeling in anyone!"

"That just isn't true," Ardell said emphatically. "You've been unlucky."

Chapter Fifteen

The week with her parents passed quickly. Gilyan told them about the destroyed project, and they co-operated by giving her the privacy necessary to re-do her lost writing.

No word had been mentioned of Jay, and she volunteered nothing about Phil Randall. For some reason, Gilyan felt a deep sense of shame connected with both.

On Saturday afternoon, Gilyan discussed with her father the re-done project on Opera for Everyone. He thought it an excellent idea.

"You get Mrs. Darlinger's agreement to come back in as a sponsor and you'll have it made." The gray eyes narrowed. "Incidentally, why didn't you go after her earlier? What if you've done all this work and she isn't interested?"

"I intended seeing her, but Julia said Mrs. Darlinger was in Europe and wouldn't be back for a couple of weeks, which should put her back in town about the time I am."

"Who told you that?"

"Julia. Julia Caldwell."

"Well, Julia's very much mistaken. Mrs. Darlinger came back from Europe over a month ago."

"Oh, no! How did Julia make such a mistake? Well, I'll see her as soon as I get back. Do you know her?"

Malcolm Barr nodded. "I certainly do, and I'll give you a letter to her. Perhaps it will help."

With renewed vigor that Saturday night, Gilyan tackled the finishing touches on her promotional campaign.

Her parents had gone out for the evening and Gilyan, in slim green pants and a bulky sweater of the same green, was curled up in a corner of the living room before the fire, proofreading, when the hall chimes sounded. Reluctantly, she stopped reading and, still carrying a sheaf of papers, walked to the door and threw it open.

A very tall young man with craggy features and light-gray eyes stood there looking down at her. Above the cleft chin, the well-molded mouth parted in a dazzlingly white smile.

Gilyan thought she had gone crazy. The hallway tilted, her throat felt dry, her knees turned to liquid. With a whispering sound, the papers in her inert hand cascaded to the heavy foyer carpet.

Fortunately, he spoke first. Gilyan was incapable of uttering a word.

"Gilyan! This is nice." Rob reached out and took one of her limp hands.

"R-Rob?" she managed, and decided that she really had taken leave of her senses. She wanted to fling her arms around the wide shoulders, to laugh and cry at the same time. If this was madness, then it was a wonderful, warm madness. She was actually trembling with it.

Before she could move, Rob was bending and picking up the spilled papers, and in those few seconds, Gilyan managed to get herself in hand.

"May I come in?" Rob said, smiling down at her.

"Oh, yes, yes! I'm—I'm just so glad to see you!" The words were pretty pallid compared to the extent of her gladness.

Rob sat down in the big blue chair and she sat across from him. "I can't stay," he was saying in the remembered soft, deep voice. "I'm going down to San Francisco tonight."

"I'm going down tomorrow," Gilyan said eagerly, hoping that he would suggest their going down together. But he didn't.

The crisp brown hair, still showing a tendency to wave, nodded toward the window. "I have someone waiting in the car."

Instantly, some of Gilyan's glow departed. Was it a girl? She *was* insane! This was Rob. Rob

Hunter, who used to care for her, who had given her every chance to reciprocate his feelings. Despair took possession of Gilyan. Jay and Phil were shadow emotions. How stupid could she have been? Rob was looking at her questioningly, and she managed to speak coherently.

"Rob—I—can't tell you how exciting I think your column is, nor how surprised—and delighted —I was when I heard that you were The Lamplighter. Why didn't you ever let me know?"

The remembered, long-fingered hands reached into a pocket to pull out cigarettes. The white smile flashed as he proffered the package. "I guess it was because I yelled playwright into your long-suffering ear so often, how I wasn't going to settle for anything less."

"But Rob, your column is read all over the country. It's marvelous satire."

"Well, thank you," he said easily, and Gilyan wondered how she had ever been so misguided as to think Rob gauche. She had mistaken quietness for unsurety!

"I understand Matt Groody is to carry your column?" she said.

"Yes. That's one reason I'm going to San Francisco. I have an appointment with Matt and Mrs. Groody on Monday."

Faintly, Gilyan heard the sound of a horn. Rob was instantly on his feet. Gilyan jumped to hers and put out a protesting hand. "You're not going?"

"Yes. As I said, someone's waiting for me in the car and we're flying down tonight." Was it a man or a woman, waiting in the car? Rob added, "Shall we have dinner together, Monday night, in the city?"

Gilyan controlled the wild wave of elation. "I'd like that very much. Wait till I get you my address." She turned toward the desk.

"I have it," Rob said. "You wrote me, remember?"

Gilyan flushed. "I enjoyed hearing from you. Well . . ." She could think of nothing further to say. Rob's light-gray eyes were friendly, nothing more, as he turned.

"I'll see you Monday night. I may see you earlier in the day at the *Globe,* too. Good night, Gilyan. Give my very best to Malcolm and Karen. I'll visit with them when I come back."

When Gilyan's parents came in, Gilyan was sitting woodenly on the couch before the fire, watching the dancing flames. Tears had dried on her face.

"Gilyan!" Her mother stood before her. "What's the matter, honey?"

Gilyan's chin shook, but her tone was even. "Frankly, I'm ashamed to tell you."

"Tell us what, Chicken?" her father said, dropping into the blue chair.

"Rob was here," Gilyan said flatly. "And the moment I saw him at the door," her voice wobbled, steadied, "I—I got all shook up! I—I can't understand myself! Am I—some kind of a freak?"

Her mother smiled and sank back in relief. "You're not a freak," she said.

"But Mother," Gilyan leaned forward, "what ails me? I thought my heart was broken over Jay. Fortunately, Jay jilted me. I say fortunately, because the last time I saw him I realized I hadn't loved him as I thought I did. Then Phil—Dr. Randall—starts showering me with attentions and, even though I didn't care for him in that way, if *he* hadn't changed his mind, too, I might have learned to care for him! Then Rob . . ." Her words tumbled over one another, her face pale and tear-streaked. "I see Rob and my heart feels as if there were an explosion. What *ails* me!"

"Gilyan," her mother said placidly, "your father and I always felt that deep down—in that waiting heart of yours—you cared for Rob, but felt that everyone was pushing him at you. Everyone—including your father and me, and Rob himself. He was always around. We both felt —and I might add, hoped—that being apart would do the trick. We didn't figure on two things: Rob's rigid pride, when he wouldn't write you and wouldn't let us tell you what he was doing, and the fact that Jay Hanover was going to enter your life at that time." Her mother's hands flew out. "Simple."

"I don't see anything simple about it!" Gilyan stormed. "Rob looked at me like I was a pleasant little playmate from out of his past."

"How did you *expect* him to look at you?" Her father asked dryly. "We haven't had close contact with Rob, either. We've been pretty far away, remember? We don't know how the boy feels about you now. If you're lucky. . . ."

"He's—changed. He seems so sure of himself." Gilyan sounded forlorn.

"That does it!" Her father's eyes were stern. "Isn't that exactly what you always wanted? Rob to change? Now wait a minute—" He flung up a hand as Karen started to interrupt.

"We've discussed Jay Hanover's emotional immaturity and I think it's about time to discuss one facet of *yours*. You are an intelligent, sensible girl, and we love and admire you very much. However, you do seem to lend a helluva lot of importance to what you call 'sophistication' and polish. Just what is this blasted sophistication? A shield, a veneer that the true personality can hide behind? Usually, most likely, to conceal a pretty wobbly personality, if you ask me! Well, perhaps in *that* sense, The Lamplighter might be Rob's shield. He can say and do things in that column of his tantamount to losing inhibitions. Yet, basically, I'd be willing to bet he's the same Rob

Hunter—a nice guy who doesn't need to throw his weight around. Who might not know how to order your dinner from a French menu, but would be like the Rock of Gibraltar in a time of crisis." He grinned suddenly. "Okay, I've had my say."

"And quite enough, I'd say," Karen said. "The best thing we can do is keep out of the whole thing."

Malcolm Barr rose. "I need a drink. Women!" he muttered, and walked out of the room.

Gilyan looked at her mother. "Daddy's right. B-but I really couldn't help it." she said, sounding like a small child. "I—really couldn't." Tears welled in the luminous hazel eyes.

Karen touched her daughter's hand. "Honey, you know how you feel now. All you can do is hope that Rob feels the way he used to. Frankly, I've always thought Rob one of the most stable people I ever knew. However, I must admit that two years is a long time. Just keep your chin up."

All the way back on the plane, Gilyan wondered if she was keeping her chin up, or sticking it out. Yet she was certain of one thing: If Rob had lost all interest in her, if he had learned to care for someone else, there was absolutely no one to blame but herself.

Tomorrow seemed a thousand light years away.

Chapter Sixteen

When Gilyan reached the *Globe* office on Monday morning, she was surprised to find Hannah pacing the floor of her office, looking even more disheveled than usual. As Gilyan spoke from the doorway, Hannah whirled around.

"Gilyan! I've been waiting for you," she exclaimed. "Where on earth have you been?"

Gilyan was surprised. "You asked me to go down to the . . ."

"Never mind—I remember!" Hannah grabbed Gilyan's arm and practically dragged her into Gilyan's office and closed the door. Gilyan just had time to get one swift look at newly painted walls, a new desk and waxed floors before Hannah was talking.

"You've been scooped!" she wailed. "Julia Caldwell came up with a promotional idea that

Matt's ecstatic about. Julia didn't tell me she was working up a campaign—and what struck her to do one at this time, I can't imagine. But Gilyan, yours would have to be a real blockbuster to beat Julia's!"

Gilyan sank down in the chair behind her new desk. "When did all this happen?"

"While you were away. Julia said she'd been working on the idea for ages and just got it finished. Remember while she was away—just before you left for Oregon—with the flu? She said she did the final touches then. Even got Mrs. Darlinger to sponsor . . ."

Gilyan sat up. "Wait a minute. What *is* her idea?"

Hannah ran fingers through her tousled hair. "You know how badly the opera's been going? The attendance off and Mrs. Darlinger pulling out? Well, Julia got this terrific idea of putting on a side opera—so to speak—for everyone. She calls it, Opera for All." Hannah, too disturbed to notice the incredulous look growing on Gilyan's face, continued: "She'll do interviews with the conductors, with the performers, and have presentations that don't call for the usual formal dress. Scaled-down tickets. Mrs. Darlinger is very enthusiastic and Matt is all ready to go to town on it. You know what that'll mean when I tell Matt I'm leaving?" Hannah's look suddenly sharpened. "What's the matter? You're white as a sheet."

Gilyan felt sick. She was recalling the disturbed way her notes had looked when she opened the desk drawer and found the big clip missing. The fire . . . How had Julia managed that? Julia was at home sick with the flu when the fire occurred. Yet she knew, as surely as if she had seen her set the match, that somehow Julia had managed the fire. Julia telling her that Mrs. Darlinger was in Europe when she wasn't. Julia had been planning even then to take Gilyan's campaign. And where did Gilyan stand? She had none of the original notes. Only the re-done copy she had brought back from Oregon. Gilyan had never mentioned the idea to Ardell because of her promise to Hannah; and not to Hannah herself, because Hannah was only interested in seeing the completed project. Where did that leave her? She had discussed the project with her father, but that wouldn't carry much weight, would it? She looked up at Hannah.

"Where is Julia?"

Hannah jerked her head. "In her office. Why?"

Gilyan didn't answer, but rose and walked out of her office and into Julia's. The blonde head was bent over a ream of scattered papers. Softly, Gilyan closed the door and leaned against it. "Julia . . ."

The blonde head came up. The amber eyes lighted as they saw Gilyan. "Oh, Gilyan! It's nice to see you. How was your vacation?"

Gilyan stared in disbelief. The beautiful amber

174

eyes were wide and clear above the smiling mouth. For a second, Gilyan wondered if it was remotely possible that Julia had, by a wild stretch of coincidence, come up with the same idea as hers at the same time. Then, under her prolonged look, something flickered deep in the amber eyes.

Slowly, Gilyan walked to the desk and leaned her hands on it. "Why, Julia? Are you so determined to get ahead, to make that dream of yours come true, that you'd plagiarize?"

Pink touched the clear complexion. "What *do* you mean, Gilyan?"

Another fragment of memory clicked in Gilyan's mind. "You were listening when Hannah told me she was leaving the first of the year and suggested that I do a promotional campaign." It wasn't a question but a statement. Hannah had thought someone was listening outside Gilyan's office door. And when she got up to look, the door had been ajar.

"I don't know what you're talking about, Gilyan, but I must say, I never thought you'd be a poor loser."

Fury caught Gilyan by the throat. "You must want to be a columnist pretty badly to stoop to plagiarism! You know, and I know, you've taken my whole idea in one fell swoop. *You* managed to set that fire . . ."

Julia's rosy mouth parted. "Why, Gilyan, what

a thing to say! I wasn't even here the day of the fire."

Another piece clicked into place. Elmer's expression, his almost belligerent reply to Gilyan's question, the day of the fire. The way he had flushed and hurried off. "What did you do? Have poor, besotted Elmer set it for you?"

A wave of telltale color swept the face before her, then receded.

"Can you prove it? Can you prove I stole your idea? Do you have any notes or papers to show that it *was* your idea?"

Gilyan tapped the manila envelope she held. "The whole thing is right here."

Julia smiled. "And when did you do that? I told by idea to Matt *while you were away.*"

So it was "Matt" now. Gilyan straightened, but before she could speak, the girl across the desk suddenly changed. A look of distress crossed her face, the amber eyes filled yith tears. "Why, Gilyan, I'm surprised and hurt, I can't *imagine* you accusing me of stealing an idea of yours. I—I've worked on this campaign for *weeks.* I've spent night after night, doing research. I can't imagine you saying—even thinking—my idea of Opera for All is yours." She lifted a pleading hand. "Gilyan, dear, what can you *possibly* hope to gain by such a maneuver? I've always been so fond of you —trusted you so!"

Gilyan stared down at the blonde girl in bewilderment, feeling as if she were watching a performance. Suddenly she turned her head. Rob Hunter was standing in the doorway. It *had* been a performance—for the man Julia saw in the doorway at Gilyan's back.

Julia, looking startled, jumped to her feet. "Oh, Mr. Hunter! I didn't see you. We're in a very distressing situation here." With pretty helplessness, Julia chocked a bit, then continued: "You heard about my promotional campaign?"

Rob nodded. "Mr. Groody was telling me about it."

"Well," Julia spread her hands appealingly, "Gilyan says it is hers, and . . ."

Quietly, Rob interrupted: "I see. My suggestion would be to go in and see Mr. Groody. All of us."

Julia astonished Gilyan by instantly agreeing. "Yes! Right now." She was acting very sure of herself, and yet Gilyan felt convinced that Matt would most certainly be open to hearing her side. If anything, he would tend to lean to her side. So why was Julia so ready, so eager, to go in to see him?

Gilyan felt encased in a block of ice as they walked down the hall to Matt's office and passed Vida's desk. Rob hadn't so much as looked Gilyan's way. As Rob opened Matt's inner door, Gilyan heard a woman's voice, raised and angry, but quickly cut off as they appeared. It was Alice

Groody, looking ill and very upset. She turned her back to them and walked over to the window.

Matt stood up. "Mr. Hunter—girls—won't you sit down?" Uncomfortably, Gilyan sat. Julia looked demure, and serenely confident.

"Alice," Matt said to the silent figure by the window, "would you wait outside for a few minutes?"

Surprisingly, the dark head shook. "I'm comfortable where I am."

Matt's heavy brows lowered, but he didn't press the point. He looked around, then his eyes settled on Julia. "Do you want to begin?" This gave Gilyan a small flicker of surprise. Matt acted as though he knew an issue was at stake, that she and Julia were here to be heard on that issue. How could this be? Even Hannah hadn't been aware that Julia's promotional campaign was Gilyan's.

"I don't know if you would be interested, Mr. Groody," Julia spoke softly, "but I've always wanted to work my way up to doing a column or work on a woman's page like Miss Davis does. One day," she turned apologetic eyes on Gilyan, "I couldn't help but overhear Gilyan and Miss Davis conspiring—I mean, talking—about getting Gilyan Miss Davis's job when she left. So, I thought that even though Gilyan had the inside track, with Miss Davis's sponsorship, I would try a promotional campaign myself. I heard her suggest that Gilyan try one . . ." Prettily, she hesitated.

"Go ahead, Miss Caldwell," Matt said. Gilyan could read nothing in his tone. Rob was silent and the woman by the window didn't seem to be paying any attention to the people in the room behind her.

"Well," Julia went on, "I remembered that the opera attendance had been hitting the news a lot lately and I thought I would pick just such a topical subject for my campaign. San Franciscans love their opera and we need to get more people attending. My idea for doing that is there, on your desk. Unfortunately," the amber eyes filled, "Gilyan is trying to say my idea is hers. How she can say this, I can't imagine! I have notes from two weeks back when I started this promotional idea. Why—why," a few of the tears spilled over, "she even accused me of setting fire to her desk, when I wasn't even in the building!"

Matt's face had slowly turned the color of brick. He started to turn to Gilyan, then abruptly turned back toward the woman at the window. "Alice, I think it would be best if you waited outside. You can't be interested in this little rhubarb."

His wife turned and gave him a long look. "I am very interested," she said, and again turned back to stare out of the window.

Matt's flush deepened as he turned to Gilyan. "May I hear your side of this?" he asked.

Trying to speak slowly, to keep a checkrein on her temper, Gilyan filled him in. She told him how Hannah had sworn her to secrecy because she wanted to be the first to tell Matt when she would be married. She explained how Hannah had thought someone was listening, but when she opened the door, she saw no one. She explained, acutely conscious of Rob's intent regard as she talked, how her papers had been burned so that she had to rewrite the whole thing during her week in Oregon. To Gilyan's own ears, she didn't sound nearly so convincing as Julia had.

"Bosh, Gilyan!" Matt snorted. "That fire was started by a cigarette being thrown in the wastebasket." His eyes fell on Rob. "I'm sorry, Hunter. I didn't mean to keep you in on this little fuss. Would you rather wait for me in the outer office?"

Rob shook his head and straightened in the chair. "Oh, no. In fact, I may have a small bit to contribute."

Gilyan's hazel eyes fastened on Rob. What did he mean? She was beginning to feel there was little meaning in any of this. A knot seemed to be forming in her midsection. Matt's reaction was very different from what she had expected. It had never occurred to her that he wouldn't be fair, that he wouldn't see the truth. His next words rocked her back.

"Gilyan—Julia—I try to stay out of personality clashes in my business. However," he turned to Gilyan, "the only way I can see to resolve this is to go along with the one whose plans are the more advanced. After all, Julia's are completed and turned in. She has already seen Mrs. Darlinger and has her sanction. You should know, after a lifetime with writers, that many come up with the same idea at the same time."

Gilyan couldn't believe her ears. She caught a flash of complacency on Julia's face; then Rob was speaking, quietly and firmly.

"Writers *do* come up with the same ideas simultaneously, Mr. Groody, but hardly in such minute detail." He reached into an inner pocket. "It just so happens that I have a letter here from Gilyan, dated *before* Miss Caldwell says she started her promotional campaign, telling me in detail about her plan for Opera for Everyone. Would you like me to read it?" He kept his eyes on Matt.

Before Matt could reply, Julia was on her feet. "That's a lie! Can't you see he's in love with her and would say anything to get her off the hook? They've known each other for ages. Can't you . . ."

"Get-out-of-here!" The sharp, distinct words came from Alice Groody and were directed at Julia.

Julia whirled, and Alice started stiffly forward, her face distorted with hate. "You-get-out-of-here!

181

Out of this building! Out of my sight. Don't ever come *near* the *Globe* again!"

Julia, white-faced, a hand to her mouth, was slowly backing away from the fury of the older woman.

"Don't you think I know about you and Matt?" Alice demanded. "Do you think I didn't know he was paying for that fancy apartment on Vista Street? That they know you at the apartment building as Mrs. Julian Carter, whose husband has to travel a great deal in his business? Do you think I didn't know about all those expensive clothes? The jewelry?" Alice's voice abruptly flattened, became dead sounding. Gilyan wanted to put her hands over her ears, but she couldn't move. From the corner of her eyes, she saw Rob looking intently down at the carpeting. "Matt's had affairs before," the dead-sounding voice continued, "but he always came back to me. This one," the voice again rose, "has lasted just too long! He's getting a choice right now. It is either you—or the *Globe* and me!" She whirled, her face working.

"All right, Matt! Make your decision. Now. And frankly, it no longer matters very much what you do. I think you killed anything I might have felt for you when you sided with this lying little tramp while knowing that Gilyan was telling the truth! Why don't you go with her—now?"

Gilyan put out a blind hand and Rob suddenly

had a tight hold on it. "Let's—let's get out of here," she mumbled, and swiftly, he had an arm around her shoulder and was hurrying out of the office.

In the hallway, she leaned against the wall, shudders moving her slim frame.

Rob kept his arm tightly aroung her shoulders. "That was rough, dear. Are you all right?" The "dear" flooded her with welcome warmth. Shakenly, she smiled up at him.

"I—I think so. Rob, what's going to happen?" The hazel eyes clouded.

He shook his head. "I don't know. I really think Mrs. Groody would be better off if he left with his treacherous Julia. They make a charming pair."

Gilyan shook her head. "What a day! I feel as if someone had pulled the f-floor out from under me. First, to find out Julia was something entirely different from what I thought . . ." Again, she started to shake. "Then to walk in there convinced that Matt would know I was t-telling the t-truth . . ." Her teeth were chatering.

"Wait here," Rob said, and disappeared down the hall. Almost immediately, he was back. Ardell was with him, carrying Gilyan's coat over her arm.

"Take her home," Rob said. "I'll go in and see Miss Davis and do some explaining. I'll see you later in the day and bring you up to date."

Gratefully, Gilyan smiled up at him; then she and a bewildered Ardell left the building.

When they reached the apartment, Ardell made coffee and Gilyan filled her in on what had happened. Ardell was incredulous.

"Matt and Julia?" she gasped. "Why—why, I didn't even know they knew each other—I mean other than as boss and worker. Every time he asked her to step into his office she made a wistful production of how frightened she was! And *he* was buying all those gorgeous clothes!" As the ramifications sank home, Ardell's face firmed with anger. "What about those wealthy cousins and the sick aunt and the poor flat where she lived?"

Wearily, Gilyan shook her head. "I think we've all been had for a long time. I don't think there ever was an aunt. An invalid was a good reason to keep everyone away. I started to take Julia a book the day before leaving for Oregon and when the cab stopped at the address Marie gave me, I was sure I had the wrong place. Then when the desk clerk said they had no Julia Caldwell, I was positive Marie had made a mistake. She obviously hadn't. I suppose Julia had to give some address, and she thought no one would ever look it up. She must have moved after we sent her the fruit pack."

Ardell looked blank. "But if Matt was keeping Julia in such plush style, why did she keep on working?"

"Because," Gilyan said, "that much of what she said was true. Julia *is* determined to become a columnist."

"What do you think Matt'll do?" Ardell asked.

"I think, if he has a choice, he'll stay on as editor and say goodbye to Julia."

"How on earth did Matt and Julia manage to hide their affair from everyone at the paper?" Ardell was thinking aloud.

"Not quite everyone," Gilyan corrected. "I haven't any idea how he found out, but I'm sure Tom Monohan knew." Gilyan told Ardell what Tom had said to Vida about Julia's competition being to rich for his blood.

"You know, Ardell," Gilyan said slowly, "I couldn't care less about my campaign now. I don't think I could ever work for Matt again, much less take Hannah's job and go on as if nothing had happened. I have a thing about being falsely accused."

"I know. I was thinking while you were telling me all this—this *dirt*—that I'm glad I'll be going to join Cliff in a short time." Ardell sighed heavily. "Will you leave soon?"

"I intend to give my two weeks notice tomorrow. I think I'll go home for a while, then see what I want to do."

Somewhat timidly, Ardell said. "Gilyan, I think your Rob Hunter is a darling! Did you know he's getting a literary award on Wednesday?"

"He isn't my Rob Hunter," Gilyan said somberly. "And no, I didn't know about his getting an award. I knew there was to be a big dinner for the awards Wednesday night, but I didn't have the list."

The buzzer ripped through the apartment, and Gilyan brightened. "Get that, will you? I want to fix my face."

She tore into the bedroom and out of her beige suit. She selected a thin silk sheath of lemon yellow that seemed to cast shiny lights onto the coppery hair. Swiftly, she slipped her feet into pale aqua shantung pumps, added lipstick and went back into the front room.

Rob was sitting on the couch. As he rose, Ardell jumped up. "I have to write some letters," she said, and disappeared into her room.

Feeling unsure of herself, Gilyan walked forward. Her legs felt unsteady.

Rob's light-gray gaze never left her face. "May I have a cup of coffee?" he asked calmly.

"Oh . . . Oh, yes. Would you like to come into the kitchen while I make it?"

Rob folded his lean length behind the little pink table, making it look even smaller. Gilyan felt all thumbs as she measured out coffee, spilled it, then remeasured and finally had the coffeepot plugged in. She got out cups and saucers, then didn't know what to do with her hands. Why, she thought, hadn't she put on something with pockets!

She cleared her throat and turned, leaning against the drainboard. "What happened after I left the *Globe* today?"

Rob lighted a cigarette before answering. "I rather think Miss Julia Caldwell found her charm to be—not irresistible. I don't think there's much doubt but what Groody will choose to remain on as editor."

"I can't imagine why Alice would still want him," Gilyan said. "will she ever be able to trust him?"

Rob looked at his cigarette. "I don't know this for a fact, but I have a feeling that she knew what she was getting when she married him. It was pretty telling when she said he'd had affairs before, but always came back."

"But Rob," Gilyan exclaimed, "poor Alice is looking so dreadful, so ill. How can she bear to put up with it?"

"Love's a funny thing, Gilyan. Happiness to some—and misery to others. And some of those who are miserable wouldn't give up that misery if it meant losing the one they love." He looked up, and the gray eyes were clear. What he said next was like an electric shock.

"Not that I compare my mental make-up—even remotely—to the Alice Groodys of this world, but did you know I lived my life heart in throat and fingers crossed during the time you were going with Jay Hanover?"

Gilyan's two hands came down hard on each side of the drainboard. "Wh-what do you mean?"

Carefully, Rob snubbed out his cigarette and rose to walk over to her. He didn't touch her, just stood looking down. "I always thought, Gilyan, it was to be you and me. That singleness of thought didn't waver when I went to New York. I felt that this potentially good thing between us could withstand a separation, become better for it. You were young, and so was I. You were so used to seeing me around, I often thought you didn't see me."

Gilyan's eyes were locked on his.

"It occurred to me that there was an element of chance being taken, that you might meet someone else—and if that occurred, I was coming back. Post-haste. But you fooled me. I knew you were going around with Hanover, but it always sounded like a casual thing. And I was becoming more and more busy. When I got the news that you were engaged"—the gray eyes darkened—"I figured the gamble I made had been lost."

"How," Gilyan spoke over a dry throat, "did you know?"

Rob smiled. "I'm afraid I used your folks as a sounding board."

Gilyan's own smile was shaky. "I—I'm not surprised. They—they're awfully fond of you . . ."

"And their daughter?"

Gilyan's eyes filled, but she didn't look away. "After my idiotic behavior, how could you possibly believe me if I told you what I feel? What I felt the moment I saw you last Saturday night?"

"Try me," he said quietly.

Gilyan's face flamed. "I—I can't . . ."

"Ah, Gilyan!" Suddenly, Rob's arms were hard about her shoulders and his mouth came down on hers. The world, and everything in it, tilted. Gilyan's heart threatened to break its rib cage. When he drew back, her face was radiant.

"It's easy to say, Rob!" she cried. "I love you—very, very much—and you *know* it!"